The mystery of
the stolen painting

Ivan Kušan

The mystery of the stolen painting

Translated from the Serbo-Croatian by Drenka Willen

Illustrated by Charles Robinson

Harcourt Brace Jovanovich

New York and London

Originally published in Yugoslavia by Mladost in 1972
under the title of Koko u Parizu
First American edition

Library of Congress Cataloging in Publication Data
Kušan, Ivan, 1933–
   The mystery of the stolen painting.
   Translation of Koko u Parizu.
   SUMMARY: *Two Yugoslav boys visiting Paris become*
involved with the theft of the Mona Lisa.
   [*1. Mystery and detective stories*] *I. Robinson,*
Charles, 1931–   ill. II. Title.
PZ7.K963Myh3   [Fic]   74-24324
ISBN 0-15-243353-8

Printed in the United States of America
BCDEFGHIJK

Contents

The mystery of
the stolen painting

Paris is magnificent

I "Hands up! I've got you!" From behind him Koko heard a shrill voice. Strong, knotty fingers tightened around his neck.

He fell off the chair. "Surely," he thought, "I must be dying!"

Then he heard familiar, raucous laughter. He opened his eyes cautiously and saw the large square head of his friend Zlatko Perich.

"Scared you, didn't I?" Zlatko asked, still laughing, clearly enjoying his own joke. "Who did you think it was?"

"Very funny," Koko snapped, picking himself up slowly and with dignity.

"I've never seen anyone so scared. How are you ever going to manage in Paris, friend? You'll drop dead, you'll be so scared. You won't even have the courage to cross the street."

Paris! Koko could think of nothing but Paris. He still thought it was all a dream. Just before the school year ended—twenty days ago to be exact—Zlatko's father had called on Koko's parents to ask if Koko could accompany Zlatko on a trip to Paris. The boys would be the guests of Zlatko's uncle, a painter who lived in Paris. The summer before Zlatko had spent a month there, but this year he refused to go without his best friend and neighbor, Koko Milich.

Suspecting that the Milichs might not be able to afford the trip, Dr. Perich offered to pay for Koko's plane ticket. It *was* all like a dream. Mr. Milich agreed to let Koko go, but insisted on paying for the trip himself. It would be cheaper to take the train, but the plane was a lot simpler. The parents would take the boys to the Zagreb airport, and three hours later Zlatko's uncle would meet them in Paris.

"I wish you'd stop talking about Paris! If you don't watch out, I may even decide not to go," Koko objected as he got back on his feet, his neck still sore from Zlatko's tight grip.

"You've just got to get used to some things. Paris is no joke." Zlatko continued to tease him. "Did you do your French today?"

Koko sighed and scratched himself behind the ear. French! Of course he had studied his French! He had done nothing else the last few days. Irregular verbs! It was slow going, but he still hoped to learn something before he left. Anyway, Zlatko drilled him every day.

"Nous partons dans une semaine," Zlatko said cheerfully.

"What was that?"

"You still don't understand even the simplest sentences. We're leaving in a week—that's what I was saying."

Every day was the same. Koko studied French grammar and looked at books about Paris and France. And in the evening Zlatko would come by and drill him and tell him stories about the glories of Paris and his last year's adventures there.

This evening was no different. As Koko was reviewing the irregular verbs and admiring a large picture of Notre Dame, Paris's famous cathedral, Zlatko had crept into the room and grabbed him by the neck.

"You almost choked me, you know. It still hurts," Koko complained, feeling his neck.

"You probably think that in Paris they would do it some other way. Well, friend, that just shows how little you know about it."

Zlatko sat down, crossed his long legs, and began to tell his favorite story about Paris. Koko already knew most of it by heart, but there were always surprises. For example, who'd ever think that in Paris people came up behind you and grabbed you by the neck, as Zlatko had so clearly demonstrated.

"You really expect me to believe that?" Koko asked cautiously. "You mean they might try it the minute we get off the plane?"

"Maybe yes, maybe no," Zlatko replied cagily. "You just don't know about Paris. Every day there are some three thousand kidnappings, mostly boys our age, especially foreigners. . . . They spot a foreigner and—bang—right away. They blackmail the parents, ask for millions and millions. They just don't know when to stop. The police rush to the top of the Eiffel Tower and survey all of Paris with binoculars, looking for kidnappers. Sometimes they get them, sometimes they don't. Sometimes the kidnappers get scared and kill the victim, especially if the police are on their trail."

"You mean they can see all of Paris from the Eiffel Tower?" Koko asked excitedly.

"Why not? The Eiffel Tower is almost one thousand feet high—that's like three of our cathedrals, don't you see? Three cathedrals stacked on top of one another. With a good pair of binoculars you can see into every nook and cranny in the city."

"Cranny? What's a cranny?" Koko asked, but then he quickly lowered his head in embarrassment and scratched behind his ear.

Whenever Koko asked a silly question like this, Zlatko would leap up and pace back and forth, flailing his arms and shaking his head. Then he would get tired and collapse back into his chair. "Koko, Koko," he would say, "you don't know Paris at all. Once you've seen it, you won't talk such nonsense, I hope. Once we get to the airport there, with ten thousand planes waiting to take off . . ."

"Ten thousand! My God!" Koko exclaimed in astonishment.

Zlatko ignored this reaction, paused in the middle of the room, grabbed Koko by the neck again, and hissed violently, "Have you read Maigret?"

"No, I don't think so," Koko admitted sheepishly, knowing that he would pay for his ignorance.

"You mean to say you haven't read Simenon?"

"What Simenon? First you say Maigret, and then it's Simenon. I don't know what you're talking about."

"Simenon is a writer. Georges Simenon. A fantastic writer. And Maigret is a police inspector, a detective who solves even the most baffling cases. For example, you get off the plane in Paris—the airport is called Orly—and a sniper aims at you from the building and you get hit in the head. The police are on the scene almost instantly, photographing, measuring, asking millions of questions: How? Why? And Maigret simply lights his pipe, sits at the table, orders a glass of beer, and solves the riddle. He will immediately know who fired the shots."

"And who was it?" Koko asked softly, his eyes glued to the floor.

"Only Maigret knows," Zlatko explained cheerfully.

"But why would anybody want to shoot at us?"

Zlatko was again pacing from one end of the room to the other. This time, however, he made no reply. Explaining things to Koko seemed pointless.

Koko was still gazing at the floor. He couldn't bring

himself to ask any more questions. At first he had looked forward to the trip to Paris tremendously; now he wasn't so sure. It seemed practically impossible to survive there. He couldn't understand how Zlatko had managed to get back, alive and unhurt, last summer.

Zlatko went on with his story about the 984-foot-high Eiffel Tower, and the phantoms with black masks cruising the streets at night, and the hundreds of bridges over the river Seine, which was so wide that you couldn't see across it, about the blindmen who shoot at passersby with their metal canes, and the cripples who have machine guns and radio transmitters built into their wooden legs, and the movie stars who sit at street corner cafés drinking Coca Cola.

"Is this cathedral beautiful?" Koko asked, picking up the photograph of Notre Dame, hoping to divert Zlatko from the horrors awaiting them in the French capital.

"Of course it's beautiful," Zlatko said. "*And* dangerous!" he added in a deep, awesome voice.

"Why dangerous, Zlatko?"

"It's an ancient cathedral, full of cellars and secret passageways that no one dares take a peek at. Besides, it's a well-known fact," said Zlatko, lowering his voice to a whisper and narrowing his eyes, "that the bell ringers of Notre Dame are hunchbacked monsters who spend their nights looking for victims, attacking them . . ."

Koko retreated into a corner, he was so frightened. "How can your uncle live there? Isn't he scared?" he asked.

"Scared?" Zlatko sounded surprised. "He's a painter, you know. And all painters are a bit odd," Zlatko said, placing his finger on his forehead and twisting it significantly.

"Ah, well," Koko whispered, as if he finally understood. He looked out of the window. His eyes fell on his favorite locust tree. It looked so friendly in front of his bedroom window. Koko suddenly felt sorry that he was going to leave his old house, his parents and yard, and that locust tree down there. How could one possibly enjoy the thought of a trip to a new, magnificent city if passengers got shot in the middle of the forehead the minute they got off the plane?

"You should go to bed," Zlatko said with great seriousness. "Get a lot of rest before the trip. You've never been on a plane before, and it might upset you. Some people have to be carted off to the hospital right from the airport. You really should get a lot of rest. Get up early tomorrow morning and review your French grammar. What's the present tense of the verb *faire?*"

"*Je fais, tu fais . . .*" Koko stammered in despair, scratching behind his ear.

Zlatko finally left. Koko quickly said good night to his parents and sister and crawled into bed. The locust tree swayed gently in front of his window.

"Survival is what counts," Koko thought just before he fell asleep. "If I'm careful, I may make it. Come back from Paris alive. . . . And when I tell my friends . . ."

The most valuable painting in the world

2 Seven days passed like seven minutes in a dream. Dr. Perich drove the boys to the airport in his car. Koko's mother and sister came along. Everyone smiled bravely. Koko had never been far away from home, nor had he ever been on a plane. When they were safely on board, Koko secretly wiped away a couple of tears.

"See how small the houses are?" Zlatko asked when the plane took off.

"Yes, yes, I see," Koko said softly. He pretended to look down, but he kept his eyes tightly shut.

"Sometimes hawks fly right into the engines and can't get out. The engines stop, and—crash!"

Koko was silent. He was trying not to listen. If hijackers and thunderstorms didn't get them first, surely they would hit a mountainside in the fog, or else the landing gear wouldn't work.

By the time they reached the Paris airport, Koko's ears were buzzing and he felt very dizzy. He saw what seemed like ten thousand planes, glistening like fish in a pond. They entered the arrivals building, which was as large as ten stadiums.

"There's my uncle! Hey, Uncle!" Zlatko yelled and pulled Koko along through the crowd.

"No one has taken a shot at us!" Koko thought happily. "Zlatko must be exaggerating. It must be all those books . . ."

"This is my best friend Ratko Milich, but we call him Koko."

"Delighted to meet you!" Zlatko's uncle exclaimed cheerfully and shook Koko's hand.

The boy looked him over carefully to see if he was as crazy as Zlatko said he was. He could see nothing unusual: dark hair, thin beard, narrow face, a French beret. The only striking feature was a prominent scar on his cheek.

"It's great to be here again, Uncle! Let's go into the city right now. Koko must see the Eiffel Tower this minute, and the Arc de Triomphe, and Napoleon's tomb, and the zoo, and Notre Dame, and the Seine . . ."

"Shhhh," his uncle whispered, a finger on his mouth as he glanced around. "First I must show you something . . ."

As they walked over to the bus stop, Zlatko grabbed Koko's arm and whispered into his ear, "Well, didn't I tell you?"

Koko was speechless. The bus sped through the southern suburbs of Paris, hit heavy traffic, then passed by a huge stone lion perched in the middle of a square, turned toward the river, and finally stopped in front of a domed building, which Koko was sure was a church.

"That's Napoleon's tomb!" Zlatko said proudly, as if referring to a close friend.

"Why such a gigantic grave? I thought Napoleon was small, like a dwarf . . ."

"Let's get moving, boys. Faster!" Zlatko's uncle mumbled as they ran down a flight of stairs. They were entering the Paris subway.

"I thought we were going to Napoleon's tomb," said Zlatko, disappointed.

"Shhhh," Zlatko's uncle continued, a finger on his lips. "Later, later, tomorrow. . . . First I want to show you something you've never seen before in your life . . ."

Koko looked at Zlatko in amazement. Zlatko nudged him in the ribs. They were waiting on the platform. The train arrived, and all the doors opened at once with a hiss. The three rushed into the train, the doors banged shut, and the train roared through the underground tunnels so fast that they had to hold onto their seats.

"What do you say?" Zlatko asked triumphantly. "Not like our streetcars, is it?"

"I'll say it isn't," Koko replied. It was hot and stuffy.

"All right, boys, tumble out," his uncle said at the next stop.

But they didn't leave the subway. They changed trains, rode another five stops, then walked for about ten minutes through endless corridors and got on still another train. Koko thought how horrible it would be to get lost in Paris. They rode for a while on a fourth train and then got into a big elevator at a station called Pelleport. When the heavy iron doors opened at last, they were on the street. Koko took a deep breath. Cars were speeding furiously along the wide street, and the air smelled as if they were in a garage.

"It's nice in my neighborhood here," Zlatko's uncle said. "Quiet. No commotion, no noise, much better than in the center of the city."

"Better than the center of the city?" Koko thought. "What must it be like there if we can barely hear one another talking here?"

Zlatko led the way. He remembered it from the year before. First a right turn, then a left, and then they were on a small and relatively quiet street called Bretonneau. The painter lived at 3 Rue Bretonneau. Koko remembered the address because last year he had written Zlatko a letter at this place.

"Shhhh," Zlatko's uncle hissed again, looking carefully behind him as he shoved the boys inside the entry way. The three climbed a long flight of creaky wooden stairs, which at last brought them to a door on which it said Poklé.

"That's what they call me in Paris!" the painter whispered as he unlocked the door.

His apartment was small and modestly furnished. At one end a flight of rickety stairs led up to an attic. The painter was now crawling about on the floor, turning a pot right side up, squeezing under the bed, looking behind a wall clock, and removing a floor board. Each one of these hiding places contained a key. Armed with the four keys he climbed up into the attic. The boys' eyes glistened with excitement. Zlatko nudged Koko in the ribs. Indeed, Uncle Poklé must be out of his mind. What other reason would there be for the quadruple locking of an attic door?

The attic was dark and very messy: piles of rags, picture frames, paint brushes, old newspapers, dried-up paints, and oil smudges. A heavy black curtain hung on the wall opposite the window.

"Are you hungry, boys?" asked the painter, and, clearly not interested in their answer, walked over to the black curtain. "Now get ready to see something the like of which you've never seen before in your lives! One, two, three!"

He pulled back the black curtain; behind it was an equally heavy red curtain. He pulled the red curtain back, revealing a white one. The painter pulled that one back, and the boys saw before them a painting of a beautiful young woman sitting with her hands in her lap, smiling mysteriously.

"The *Mona Lisa!*" Zlatko screamed.

"What did you say?" Koko yelped.

"Bravo, Zlatko! You recognized it right off. You see before you the most famous portrait ever painted, the *Mona Lisa* of the immortal Leonardo da Vinci. The most

famous painting in the world, boys, and the most valuable."

"How come," Zlatko began nervously, "how come it's here? . . . The *Mona Lisa* hangs in the museum, in that museum—what is it called?—the Louvre. How come you've got it here?"

"Quiet!" the painter yelled, suddenly dropping the three curtains and putting his hand on Zlatko's mouth. "It's a secret—a secret on which my entire future depends. No one knows about it yet, except for you two. . . . Come!"

The painter pushed the two boys out onto a small balcony. Koko suddenly realized how many flights they had climbed. Paris spread—mysterious, endless—into the distance.

Koko knew nothing about the *Mona Lisa* or Leonardo. But Zlatko watched his uncle in absolute disbelief, and when his uncle removed his hand from his mouth, Zlatko asked softly, "Did you really steal the *Mona Lisa?*"

"Shhh!" The uncle hissed and banged the balcony railing so hard that two upright posts came loose. "I'll explain everything. I don't want anyone else to know about it, you understand."

"Why can't we see the Eiffel Tower from here if it's as tall as you say, Zlatko?" Koko began, but his friend stopped him cold.

"Shut up, Koko!" Zlatko yelled. "How can you be so naive? Didn't you hear what my uncle said? This is no game, no child's play . . ."

The most valuable painting in the world [27]

"I know, Zlatko. This is the *Mona Lisa*."

"*Mona Lisa*, he says!" Zlatko rolled his eyes and clenched his fists. "You haven't the slightest idea of what the *Mona Lisa* is all about."

"I'll explain everything," his uncle whispered again. "Everything. But it's a deadly secret. As I said, my whole future is tied up in it, you know. If I make a lot of money, as I suspect I will, I can paint anything I want, don't you see? Anything I want, and not just what I am commissioned to. I'll paint huge suns. Look at that glorious sun up there! What color is the sun? Blue! A large blue sun! If I'm successful, I'll only paint blue suns. . . . But, if I'm not . . ."

"What will you do then?" Zlatko sounded very concerned. "What will you do then, Uncle?"

"I'll climb to the very top of the Eiffel Tower—and jump."

"Oh, no," Koko cried, putting his hand to his mouth.

Zlatko grabbed his uncle by the beard, looked him straight in the eyes, and asked solemnly, "Uncle, did you really steal the *Mona Lisa*—the most valuable painting in the whole wide world? Uncle, you are mad! You'll never be able to sell it."

"Shhhh," the painter said, once again putting his finger to his lips. His face was twisted.

Koko began to realize that his trip to Paris, to which he had looked forward so much, would be more exciting and dangerous than the most dreadful dream.

The most famous journalist in France

3 Marie Cléver stood in front of the mirror, admiring herself. She smoothed down her lovely hair, smiled at her reflection, stared into her own large gray eyes, and sat down on the couch.

She had every reason to be happy. School was over, and her father had promised to take her to the seaside for vacation, where she just might meet one of those very same actors whose photographs lined the walls of her room. Her own room! Yes, ever since they moved into their large new apartment on the Rue Erlanger, she had had her own room, which she could furnish any way she wanted to. She had filled it with pictures of famous actors and actresses and with books about spies. She loved spy stories.

However, there was one thing that worried her: the way her father treated her. He simply couldn't accept the fact that soon she would be thirteen years old, which is to say a grown-up, mature girl. He still treated her as if she were five years old.

Marie Cléver sighed and reached for the newspaper. It was the afternoon edition of *Le Clairon du Soir* for which her father worked. He was probably one of the most famous journalists in all of France. People snapped up copies of the paper like hot cakes every time Marcel Cléver had an article in it.

"Father!" The girl suddenly remembered and rushed to the door. She ran through every room in the house, but no one was there except their housekeeper and Leo, the old cat. Her mother was in Switzerland, and her father. . . . Ah, well, he had failed once again to keep his promise: to introduce her to Alles Worson, the famous actor-director now making a new film in Paris with Veronica Mitty and Tom O'Pool.

"I'll show him yet!" Marie tried hard to hold her tears back. "I'll show him. He thinks I'm still a baby, playing with dolls or something. I've asked him so many times to take me to his office. He knows how much I'd love it. I know he won't take me to the Louvre tomorrow to watch the shooting. . . . He doesn't think I could write for *Le Clairon du Soir*. But I could! Better than he, I'll bet. About actors, about spies—about everything. I'll surprise him yet."

Marie Cléver sat down and picked up the paper again. She reread her father's article. It was very exciting, and he certainly knew how to pick a good title.

THE THEFT OF THE *Mona Lisa* FROM THE LOUVRE

As we all know, the most valuable painting in the world, Leonardo da Vinci's portrait of Mona Lisa Gioconda, has hung in the Louvre for many, many years. In the last century there have been several attempts to steal it. However, only one was successful. Before World War I, an Italian patriot managed to remove the painting from the Louvre and smuggle it into Italy. His intention was not to become rich—he would not have been able to sell it anyway—he simply wanted to bring the painting back to his country, where he felt it belonged. Tomorrow the theft of the *Mona Lisa* will again take place at the Louvre, but this time on the screen . . .

"Splendid!" Marie exclaimed in excitement. "My father writes so well. To begin with, you don't really know what he's getting at: perhaps the *Mona Lisa* was stolen again . . ."

A film is being shot in Paris called *A Million-Dollar Painting,* directed by the famous American actor-director Alles Worson. It closely follows the story of the theft of the *Mona Lisa* by the Italian who took it back to his own country and had it hanging above his bed. His best friend realized that the painting was the original from the Louvre, and so the thief bound him with ropes and held him under the famous painting and practically let him starve to death for fear he would give him away. . . . It is widely believed that tomorrow . . .

For the hundredth time the girl looked with admiration at the picture of Alles Worson, with his huge black beard and his opaque sunglasses.

"If only my father had remembered," she thought sadly. "But I'll show him yet who his daughter is."

Meanwhile, Marcel Cléver was making his way in his Citroën through the thick Paris traffic toward Avenue de la Bourdonnais, in the vicinity of the Eiffel Tower, where Worson had secretly rented an apartment for the duration of his stay in Paris.

"I'm sorry I didn't bring Marie with me," Cléver thought as he drove. "She must be very angry, but I really couldn't. . . . Business is business, and she is much too young to be dragged into my journalistic escapades. Besides, Alles Worson would be angry if I brought another person. I am the only journalist he gave his address to . . ."

Cléver parked on Rue Camou and walked over to Avenue de la Bourdonnais. He had promised Worson he would try not to attract attention. Above all, the great actor-director wanted to protect his privacy.

He rang the bell at 23 Avenue de la Bourdonnais. Worson's private secretary, a tall woman with gold-rimmed glasses, opened the door.

"I'm sorry," said the secretary, blocking the entrance, "Mr. Worson is not receiving anyone. Who gave you the address? It's a secret."

"Tell Alles that Marcel's here. He'll receive me, I'm sure."

The secretary surveyed the visitor from head to foot.

She could sniff out a journalist from three miles away.

But when she returned a few minutes later, she was wearing a smile that was brighter than the gold frames of her glasses.

"Mr. Worson's waiting for you," she said cordially and bowed.

Alles Worson, one of the most famous people in the film world, embraced Cléver warmly. The two men had met in Hollywood a few years earlier and had become good friends.

"Wonderful to see you!" exclaimed the famous man as he banged the journalist on the shoulder. He was holding a bottle of Coca Cola. As all his fans knew, he drank Coke continuously from morning to night.

"Ready?" Cléver asked and winked playfully.

"Of course. I'm ready for the craziest adventure ever, dear Marcel, and I'm happier than when I got my first Oscar. How about you?"

"One hundred percent," the journalist said with a laugh.

"You sure this'll cause an uproar?"

"An uproar that'll be the talk of Europe and America for three years, I guarantee you."

"Splendid, old man, splendid. If this contributes to the success of *A Million-Dollar Painting*, I'll make sure that *Le Clairon du Soir* becomes the most famous newspaper in the world and you the most famous journalist in the universe."

"Don't worry about that." Marcel Cléver smiled.

"Tell me, when are you scheduled to start shooting?"

"Tomorrow morning at eight sharp we meet at the Louvre. Needless to say, Veronica and Tom will be late, but so much the better. I'll ask the painter to bring the painting a little earlier, at seven forty-five. How's that?"

"Is this how you're going to be dressed?"

"Me?" Worson sounded surprised. "Well, yes. I'm always dressed this way. I never take my glasses off. And, oh, yes, I always wear this funny little yellow cap. What about you? You mean you won't have an article in tomorrow's paper?"

"Of course not," replied the journalist. "I've told my office that I'll be out of town for a couple of days. . . . They seemed a bit surprised to hear I would be away just when they start shooting your movie, but they didn't ask any questions. They think I'm onto something. Besides, I promised them a real bombshell for Monday."

The director laughed and took a swig or two from the Coke bottle. "This is going to be my most exciting adventure."

After he had seen his visitor to the door, the actor suddenly turned serious and addressed his secretary sharply.

"Linda, the shooting starts at eight, as you know. No car. Have a helicopter on the roof here at seven-thirty sharp. Don't let anyone else in."

"Yes, sir," Linda said, her white teeth flashing.

"Crack," said the parrot

4 Nikolas Somais furiously banged his cane on the floor and limped over to the other end of the room. He was not at all pleased with his son, and he could not contain his anger. And when he was upset, his leg began to hurt. He had been wounded during the war, and his legs could just barely support the weight of his heavy body.

"I won't hear of it! Absolutely not! Bicycling? No! You broke your leg once, and that's enough. And you haven't practiced the piano today at all. Do it now! Did you hear me?"

Katsarida Somais, a fourteen-year-old boy with dark hair and large green eyes, stood in front of his father with his eyes lowered. He winced every time his father raised his voice. And today that voice thundered as if it came through ten loudspeakers.

"Yes, Father, I heard you. I heard you, I did," said Katsarida softly. His father wanted to say something else, but he forgot what it was and instead banged the floor with his cane. The door opened, and Maurice, the butler, walked in timidly, his narrow eyes twinkling sheepishly above his snow-white beard and his hooked nose.

"Did the master want to see me?"

"No, no," César screeched from the window.

"He's mad!" Nikolas Somais yelled. No one could tell whether he meant his son, the butler, or the parrot.

Such was the daily routine in the household of this wealthy Greek shipowner who had made Paris his home for the last few years. His luxurious mansion was located on Boulevard de Montmorency, not far from Bois de Boulogne, the most elegant quarter of all Paris. Katsarida, the tycoon's son, repeatedly pleaded in vain with his father to let him join a bicycle club, but his father wanted Katsarida to be a musician, preferably a pianist. The other day he had thrown his cane after the boy when Katsarida said that if he had to become a musician, he would take up the electric guitar.

"May I leave?" Katsarida asked gently.

"You may, you may," the parrot screeched.

"Madmen!" Nikolas Somais yelled, banging his stick.

"The master's right," said Maurice and bowed graciously.

The fat shipowner turned around with difficulty on his good leg, looked disdainfully at Maurice, Katsarida, and César, in that order, and angrily tottered out of the room. He slammed the door with such force that the

paintings from his extensive collection danced on the walls.

"The old master's really angry. Will the young master allow me to leave the room?" the servant asked.

"No, no," the parrot announced from the window.

The boy gestured wildly and began to pace back and forth.

"I can't take it any longer. He treats me like a . . . like a parrot or something."

"Hi!" César called to him playfully.

The boy stomped over to the colorful bird and could just barely stop himself from grabbing the parrot by the tail.

"I don't know," said Katsarida. "Sometimes I think they're all against me. Even this ridiculous César's teasing me. There was a time when he wouldn't have dared to . . ."

"César has indeed changed a lot, my young master," Maurice said softly, stroking his white beard. "I've already mentioned this to the old master: he sounds as if he's gone out of his mind."

"We'll all go out of our minds in this house, my dear Maurice. You and I, and Mother, not just the parrot. . . . I don't know what's wrong with my father, Maurice. I understand that he wanted to be a painter when he was young. He paints dozens of pictures of the sea and all kinds of fishes, but they aren't worth anything. He has no more talent than this parrot here. César would have painted those pictures better with his tail. Just look!" Katsarida pointed to one of Somais's paintings—two yellow fish with enormous blue eyes. "They look like whales!"

"Well," said Maurice.

The boy suddenly stopped in the middle of the room, as if he had remembered something, and then quickly walked over to the butler who, in the meantime, had retreated into the corner.

"Maurice," said Katsarida, placing his hand on the old man's shoulder, "Maurice, you've known me since the day I was born. You wouldn't lie to me, would you? My father won't let me get anywhere near my bicycle, and he's been screaming at me more than ever. He must be terribly worried about something. Not just ordinary business worries. Maurice, you know what's bothering him, don't you? Please tell me."

"Young master, sir," the butler muttered into his beard, "I don't know, I really don't know . . . really I . . ."

"He knows, he knows!" César yelled from his cage.

"Something's truly wrong with the parrot, Master Katsarida," Maurice said, trying to change the subject. "Now he not only talks, but he understands too. He won an award. Well, he . . ."

"Maurice," the boy interrupted, "I'll bet you know more than you dare admit, more than my father suspects . . ."

"Master Katsarida, I'd tell you, really I would, if I knew . . ."

"Very well, Maurice," Katsarida said, and he heaved a great sigh, hoping to move the old butler, who loved him as much as his own children. "Very well, you don't have to tell me."

The boy walked slowly toward the door, keeping an eye on Maurice, who, he hoped, would change his mind.

"Master Katsarida," Maurice said suddenly, stroking his beard with both his hands, "as you probably know—better than I do—when the old master is preparing to launch a new transatlantic ship, he's always very excited. And this one will be his biggest—I forget how many tons."

"Each one of his ships is the biggest, Maurice. He always builds them bigger and bigger. Has he made up his mind what to name it? He always has difficulty naming his ships because they must always be named after some famous art work."

"A month ago or so, the old master . . . but that's a secret, Master Katsarida."

"Of course, Maurice, don't worry. I'd let my ears be cut off before I'd betray your trust. You know that."

"He decided to name it the *Mona Lisa*."

"The *Mona Lisa*," the shipowner's son cried in astonishment.

"Crack," cried César.

The boy started pacing back and forth, in great agitation, flailing his arms and breathing more loudly than when he rode his bike full speed along the narrow paths in the Bois de Boulogne. Then he stopped pacing, placed his hands on the old man's shoulders, and whispered, "You know, Maurice, that the *Mona Lisa* is worth millions and millions. More than five ocean liners."

"I know." Maurice's voice was now just scarcely audible, and his eyes had narrowed to two slits.

"You remember what it was like when we launched the *Cleopatra?* Father just barely saved his skin. And now it's the *Mona Lisa!* Ah, well, it's all clear now! Clear as can be, my dear Maurice. That's why he's so bad-tempered."

"Louder!" César screeched. "I can't hear you."

"That parrot's definitely out of his mind. He's joining our conversation. Did you hear him, master?"

"The *Mona Lisa!*" The boy was now talking to himself. "The *Mona Lisa!* Now we've really had it . . ."

The old butler was trying to back out of the room, casting fearful looks at the parrot and at his master's son, whose face was now as red as the parrot's neck. But Katsarida called him back.

"Maurice, I want you to make a call for me. The number is TRO 23-74. Immediately, please. Connect me in this room."

"But, Master Katsarida, you know that your father has forbidden you to have anything to do with Miss Marie Cléver, even to call her."

"I know, Maurice, I know. A shipowner's son should not keep company with a journalist's daughter. It could

prove"—and here the boy lowered his voice altogether
—"quite indiscreet. Take the *Cleopatra,* for example.
Now, Maurice, I ask you to make that call, please."

"Of course, Master Katsarida. Right away."

The old man backed out of the room, and the young
boy paused in front of the painting of the blue-eyed fish
and stuck his tongue out.

César screeched and flapped his wings.

In the corner the telephone buzzed. Katsarida quickly
picked up the receiver and said feverishly, "Marie, is that
you? Listen, I must talk to you as soon as possible. Yes,
yes, it's terribly important. My father. What did you
say? Aha. Shhhh. Good. Ring three times, twice three
times. What? Whistle? You can't whistle that loudly.
Oh, you have a whistle. But hurry up. It's terribly important . . ."

"Crack," said the parrot.

Cutthroat with scissors and razor

5 Koko understood nothing of what was happening.
   Only one thing was clear: this was not how he had imagined his visit to Paris. He had assumed they would see the Eiffel Tower and Napoleon's tomb the minute they got off the plane. Instead, Zlatko's uncle had sent them off to a barber.

"If I wanted a haircut, I could have stayed at home," Koko thought as he looked at the shadow of his thick hair sticking out in all directions. He gazed at Zlatko. His hair grew down over his ears, too. Even so, that was no reason to subject them to this merciless haircut on the very day they arrived.

"Maybe my uncle wanted to get rid of us," Zlatko said, as if guessing his friend's thoughts. "That thing with the *Mona Lisa*, that's no joke."

The boys were walking along Rue Pelleport, in the direction of Place Paul-Signac, where they had emerged from the subway earlier in the day. Zlatko knew the way well, and he was walking so fast that Koko could barely keep up with him.

"My uncle says there's a new barbershop on Avenue Gambetta. We'll find it—don't worry." Zlatko felt smug about the ease with which he was able to find his way in this new city, while Koko didn't even dare look around, let alone cross the street.

"I didn't understand what your uncle told us about the *Mona Lisa*. How will they shoot that movie, for example—and how will they exchange paintings and so on? I didn't get any of it, did you, Zlatko?" Koko suddenly stopped.

"Do you have to talk all the time, Koko? For example, for example. For example. For example, what?"

"Well, for example . . ." Koko began and swallowed. "Anyway, Zlatko, I simply don't understand. You can kill me, but I don't understand who exchanged what painting and what your uncle is going to get out of all this anyway."

"Anyway," said Zlatko and clenched his teeth in irritation, "I'll explain everything later, when we get back. I might even draw a diagram for you, but first we must get a haircut, don't you see?"

Koko scratched behind his ear and shrugged. He was clutching the money the painter had given him for the haircut and a slip of paper with his address and phone number in case they got lost.

The barbershop, which had a sign saying CHARLES'S, was empty. The owner, a tall, large man with graying hair and a wide nose, greeted them. Koko thought he looked familiar, but he reminded himself that this was this first visit to Paris and that he couldn't possibly have seen this man before.

They sat down in comfortable chairs. Zlatko explained what they wanted, and the barber got to work. Koko was first, and just as the barber was spraying his freshly cut hair with eau de cologne, a huge man with a threatening black moustache charged in. He was out of breath.

"Frédéric," the barber said. "What's the matter? Why're you so frantic? Besides, I told you . . ."

"I know, it would be better for me not to come here too often . . ." The man suddenly became aware of the two boys.

Zlatko turned toward Koko, frowned, and winked. Koko didn't have the slightest idea what that signal meant.

"Look, Charles," the visitor said. "Someone gave me a copy of *Le Clairon du Soir*, which I don't usually read, and look what it says: 'The theft of the *Mona Lisa* from the Louvre.' That's the headline! Wait, I'll skip the beginning—that's just journalistic fluff—but this here, this is very important:

Tomorrow the theft of the *Mona Lisa* will again take place at the Louvre, but this time on the screen. A film is being shot in Paris called *A Million-Dollar Painting*, directed by the famous American actor-director Alles Worson.

"Ah, well, we know that too—that's not important. Oh, yes, here it is:

It is taken for granted that precautionary measures will be taken to prevent the real theft from taking place alongside the filmed one. We all recall the disappearance of the famous Raphael painting of Cleopatra, which was later discovered by accident in a small Greek port. No one ever found out who had stolen the portrait of the famous Egyptian queen and for whom. It is not known what precautionary measures will be taken, but it is rumored that the original will be replaced by an exquisite copy by some obscure painter.

"Damn *Le Clairon du Soir!*" the barber groaned bitterly. "How did they sniff it out? Our whole plan is threatened."

Zlatko squirmed in his seat as if he were in school; Koko sat stiff as a board, pretending to understand every French word.

"What did the parrot say?" the barber suddenly asked, at which point the visitor jumped up and clapped his hand over the barber's mouth.

"Shhhh," he hissed like a snake. "Are you out of your mind? Do you have to tell everything? No wonder *Le Clairon du Soir* has all this information. Instead of blabbering, you should do something."

"Hey, I just remembered something. I keep meaning to ask you, but you don't let me get a word in edgewise. Did you say that someone *gave* you the paper? That's funny. Newspapers are not given away—they are bought, for heaven's sake. Who gave it to you?

"A cripple with a black patch over one eye," Frédéric said, suddenly feeling unsteady. "He was standing at the entrance to the Place Gambetta subway station. He handed me the paper and said, 'You might be interested in this newspaper.' By God, that's strange. It never occurred to me."

"Frédéric, Frédéric." The barber shook his head. "You'll never make a real, a real . . . you know what I mean. Come here. I have an idea that may help us get out of this mess."

The barber pulled Frédéric with him into another room, behind the curtain. They whispered there together for some time; then Frédéric suddenly rushed out, raced through the barbershop, nearly knocking over Zlatko and Koko, and darted out into the street. The barber rubbed his hands in satisfaction; then, his mind on other matters, he soaped Koko's face as if he were about to shave him.

He worked on the two boys for what seemed like hours. Zlatko thought he had never been subjected to a more awkward barber, and Koko kept wondering where he had seen him before. The more he thought about it, the more sure he was that he recognized him from a dream. What's more, Frédéric, with his black moustache, also looked familiar.

When the barber was finally through, the two boys were a sorry sight. Zlatko, with a tuft of hair on the clean-shaven top of his head, looked like a Mongolian warrior. Koko's head looked like a roll of barbed wire.

"I can't wait," said Zlatko the minute they left the barbershop. "I must tell my uncle this story. These two guys are still hoping their scheme will work out. Just think how many crooks are waiting to steal the *Mona Lisa* during the shooting! No go, though. It's out of the question. My uncle has made such a fantastic copy that Leonardo himself wouldn't be able to tell the difference. The film will be made with the false *Mona Lisa*. The real one will be somewhere deep underground, under thirty keys and locks. . . . A great guy, my uncle."

"Do you really think," Koko interrupted him, "that the barber, for example, is a crook?"

"Listen," said Zlatko, halting suddenly in front of a shopwindow. "Come here! Look at us. We look like two plucked chickens. Could this be the work of a professional barber? And in Paris, which has the best barbers in the whole wide world? Actors come here from America every day for a shave and a haircut."

"You don't mean to say this man is not a barber, do you?" Koko asked cheerfully as they were approaching Rue Bretonneau.

"Of course. A professional barber would never soap your face. You don't even have the beginning of a beard. I mean, your face is as smooth as a . . . I'd like to say as what, but it's not polite. They're gangsters, professional gangsters. But I'm not afraid of them. It's that cripple I'm scared of."

"What cripple?"

"Ah, well, the trouble is you don't understand much French. Cripple, yes. The cripple with a patch over one eye who shoved the newspaper into the moustached crook's hands. He must be quite a guy, a sly bird! Perhaps the leader of the other gang. A cripple! Do you know what that means?"

"I know, Zlatko, of course I do. A cripple is a man without a leg, for example."

"And you, Koko, you're without a head. Obviously among these gangsters a wooden leg like that is false. It probably contains a radio receiver, a pistol, and other equipment. If my uncle has anyone to fear, it's these cripples. And we'll have to help him. I feel sorry for him. He's told us three times that if he doesn't succeed, he'll jump off the Eiffel Tower."

Koko wanted to ask more questions, but he didn't dare to for fear that his friend would yell at him. One question in particular puzzled him: the painter had carefully locked the attic door in which the portrait of the *Mona Lisa* was hidden, but he had forgotten that the attic could also be reached from the other side, across the neighbor's roof and balcony, from which they had looked at Paris that afternoon. At the right time, Koko felt, he would have the courage to bring it up.

"I'll run up and see if my uncle is at home. He said he might take a quick walk while we were out. We'll wait for him and go into town together," Zlatko said. "Come on, get going. What are you thinking about?"

Cutthroat with scissors and razor [49]

"I'm thinking about the barber, for example. He asked about some parrot," Koko suddenly blurted out. "*Le perroquet*. What was that all about, Zlatko?"

"You're a parrot," Zlatko snapped at him as they climbed up the dark staircase to the painter's top-floor apartment. He suddenly paused. "Koko, you're right. The parrot is also dangerous. The cripple and the parrot. Trained parrots who peck at the victim's eyes, and a blind cripple who carries trained parrots in his false leg. That's Paris for you, my friend!"

Cold shower

6 When Zlatko got something into his thick head, there was no point in arguing with him. Koko even suspected that it may have been Zlatko who had suggested the idea of a haircut to his uncle rather than the other way around. It was hard to imagine the painter thinking of it since his own hair reached to his shoulders. And now Zlatko had made up his mind to take a shower, and all of Koko's imploring looks seeking mercy went unheeded. Zlatko had obviously made up his mind to taunt his friend by postponing the trip into town as long as possible.

"I thought," Koko finally ventured, "I thought we'd at least take a little walk. To the aquarium, to see the whales. You said there were seven of them in the pool."

"Six," said Zlatko officiously as he undressed. "We'll go. It's too late now. Tomorrow morning. We'll shower now and then go out for a walk. As soon as it begins to get dark, though, home we go."

"Why, Zlatko, why?"

"Because Paris is dangerous at night. Some beggar or other passes by, for example—that's when you use 'for example'—and offers you flowers for sale. You sniff the flowers and faint. An ambulance is on the spot within minutes—a phony ambulance, that is—and by the time you come to, you are miles away in some villa in the north of France. Meanwhile, in Paris, the kidnappers are asking for a ransom. My uncle has very little money, so they toss you off a cliff. No, my friend, no one strolls the streets of Paris at night without a revolver in his pocket."

Koko smoothed down what little hair he had left and decided to say no more. Zlatko was doing his exercises. He suddenly stopped and said to Koko, "You said you didn't understand the confusion about the *Mona Lisa*. Listen to me carefully." And Zlatko sat down on the bed, picked up an empty picture frame, and leaned it against the wall. "Look. Pretend this is the real *Mona Lisa*. It's worth millions. Now someone is making a film about an Italian who managed to steal the picture many years ago. You heard them talking about how the *Cleopatra* was stolen a couple of years ago. Also a famous painting. Thousands of people are involved in making a film. It's hard to protect the painting. Someone may steal it. Also, strong lighting may hurt it. The museum administration would never let them use too much light. Do you follow me so far?"

"Yes," Koko said in desperation.

"My uncle was fortunate to have painted the very best copy of the *Mona Lisa*. His copy will be used during the shooting. After that he has other plans for it." At that point Zlatko substituted the frame he had leaning against the wall for another one and placed the first one under the bed. "There, that's what I mean. Let's say this is now my uncle's copy. They all say that my uncle's is every bit as good as the original."

"Where will they keep the original meanwhile?"

"Ah, well, no one knows. No one is supposed to know. All those cripples and barbers would try to snap it up. For them this is the chance of a lifetime, don't you see? It's practically impossible to steal anything from a museum."

Koko finally had to admit that he understood everything. Except, of course, why they didn't simply photograph the beautiful lady. That would be simpler and cheaper, probably a perfect likeness—but he decided he would rather not ask any more questions.

While Zlatko was taking his shower, Koko took a careful look at the little door leading to the attic. He called to his friend, who was singing a little French song in the shower.

"Zlatko, can you hear me? I'd like to go up there and look at the picture."

"Don't. It's best not to," Zlatko said through the sound of the water, but then added, "Oh well, why not? If you can find all the keys. But don't stay too long because my uncle doesn't want to expose it to too much light. And don't forget to lock up afterwards."

Koko couldn't wait to get up into the attic. Not because of the *Mona Lisa,* or the *Cleopatra,* or whatever lady it was, but because he would be able to see Paris again from the balcony and Zlatko might forget about making him take a cold shower. Quickly he flipped the pot over, crawled under the bed, opened the clock, and removed the board from the floor, picking up keys at each point. He was surprised at how well he had remembered where the painter kept the keys. In a second he had all four keys and was clambering up the stairs, unlocking and removing the padlocks one after another.

Once inside the filthy attic, he had fully intended to walk straight through to the balcony. But he changed his mind. He decided to look at the mysterious painting behind the curtain after all.

"I promised Zlatko," he thought to himself, as if Zlatko would be able to tell that he had walked past the painting without even bothering to look at it.

The sun's slanting rays fell across the black curtain. Koko lifted it and noticed on the red curtain below a reflection of his own large strangely shaped head. Then he lifted the red curtain, and finally the white one. He gasped.

The *Mona Lisa* was not there. There was no painting of any kind—just a bare wall.

He flew down the stairs in three easy leaps, and the wind slammed the door shut behind him.

Zlatko was still in the shower. The water was gurgling. Koko shivered.

"Zzzzzzzzlzl . . ." Koko stammered until he finally regained his breath. "Zlatko, it's not there! Your uncle'll jump off the Eiffel Tower. . . . They've stolen it . . ."

"What are you talking about?" Zlatko yelled, turning off the shower.

"They've stolen the *Mona Lisa*," Koko finally said and slumped down on the bed.

Slowly Zlatko walked into the room. With a towel around his waist, a wavy lock of hair on top of his clean shaven head, his high cheek bones and pronounced jaw, he looked every bit an old Mongolian warrior.

"What did you say?" he asked with exaggerated calm. "What are you talking about?"

"The painting isn't there. They've stolen it. I was up there."

Zlatko gestured gently and smiled broadly.

"Koko, Koko, you're going too far. You've just hit Paris, and you think that someone has stolen a painting right out from under your nose. Come on, take a shower and cool off."

Koko shivered and scratched behind his ear.

"But the *Mona Lisa* isn't there, Zlatko, for example."

"For example, for example!" Zlatko blew up. "So what if it isn't there? Anyway, I'm going to take a look. And you go take a shower! Did you hear me?"

While Koko was taking his shirt off with trembling

fingers and thinking that not even his own mother was so merciless in forcing him into the bathtub, Zlatko slowly climbed the stairs into the attic. A moment later, Zlatko's screaming face appeared at the attic door.

"Koko! Don't you tease me. If you want to play games, look for some other fool but not me! What nonsense is this? While you're here in Paris with me, you've got to stop that funny business. No more joking."

"But, Zlatko . . ." Koko stammered in absolute astonishment.

"They've stolen the *Mona Lisa,*" Zlatko said, imitating Koko contemptuously. "And what's this thing hanging here? You tell me! Come up here."

Koko pulled his pants up as fast as he could and climbed into the attic once again. Zlatko lifted the curtains, and to Koko's great astonishment the beautiful *Mona Lisa* was mysteriously smiling again from the wall. By some miracle the painting had resumed its spot, the same old spot that had been empty just a few moments before. Koko could bet his ears it hadn't been there. He couldn't have been dreaming.

"Now I know," Koko said suddenly and rushed out onto the balcony. He looked in the direction of Pelleport and spotted a red car speeding away along Avenue Gambetta, the very same street where they had gotten those notorious haircuts earlier that day.

At the corner of Rue Bretonneau, the street Zlatko's uncle lived on, and Rue Pelleport, which led to the Métro station, Koko spotted a human figure he had never seen before but recognized all the same. The man was of medium height, his left leg was wooden, his right eye was covered with a black patch. At first the man looked in the direction of the disappearing red car, and then he slowly turned around, his glance resting on Koko and the balcony. There was no doubt about that.

"Oh!" gasped Koko, practically falling into the attic. "Oh, Zlatko, look there, outside. A red car and a . . . cripple. A cripple, for God's sake!"

Zlatko pushed his friend aside angrily.

"If you're teasing me again, old man!"

Once on the balcony again, it occurred to Koko that it might be best for him to jump from the fifth floor. The red car had vanished, and so had the cripple.

"Koko," Zlatko began through his clenched teeth, his jaw so tense that it looked as if it might crack, "Koko, I'm going to . . ."

But Koko was no longer there. In the twinkling of an eye, Koko rushed back into the attic and down the stairs, grabbing his shirt along the way, and down the main stairs into the street.

Koko had no idea where he was going or what he was doing, but he knew that for once he had to prove to his stubborn friend that he, Koko, was right—or die trying.

"Father, why are you running away?"

7   The girl put the receiver down cheerfully and shook her head. She stepped in front of the mirror again and looked at herself. She was pleased with what she saw.

"I'm sure Katsar likes me a lot," she thought to herself. The young Greek had told her that Katsar was actually his childhood nickname and meant some kind of insect. "I think I can get him to tell me all his secrets. Just like Mata Hari. Not even my father can find out as much as I can. It may teach him a lesson. I'm no longer a baby, and he might just as well know it."

With a look full of admiration she surveyed the photographs of film stars and famous spies gracing the walls of her room. Her eyes paused at the picture of Mata Hari hanging above her bed—Mata Hari, the most famous woman spy of all time, who was executed during World War I. Marie Cléver smiled with her large gray eyes, took a whistle from her closet, placed it in her blouse pocket, and walked out of the room.

The door of her father's room was ajar, which meant that he was home. Marie was surprised.

"I'll bet Alles Worson wouldn't see him. Good! Serves him right! He wouldn't take me along. I would have found a way."

She paused in front of his door. He was talking to somebody.

"My sweet little one," Marcel Cléver was saying tenderly, "we won't be together for a while. I need some rest. I'll get a haircut today, and then I'm off to the mountains for a few days. Come on, you sweet old thing, jump! Come on, Leo, jump!"

Marie shook her head in sorrow for her father. "He's talking to the cat, for heaven's sake! Of course, he may be tired and need a rest, but is that all there is to it? Perhaps there's something more serious behind it."

Marie entered the room, and the huge gray cat with orange eyes hissed furiously. The cat was jealous of the girl. Its master ignored it when the girl was around.

"Are you really going away for a few days, Papa? I can't be that little if I can stay at home without my mother and father, can I?" Marie asked sharply.

"Oh, Marie, have you been listening, you naughty girl?"

"If you can tell Leo, surely you can tell me." Marie would not be brushed aside.

Leo meowed when he heard his name mentioned and leaped on the chair.

"Marie, Marie," her father said cheerfully, walking

over to her. "Let's be friends again. I have to go to the barber. Come along. We'll take a little stroll and have a chat."

"That's odd," the girl said. "Why would you be having your hair cut all of a sudden. That's big news. They should have it on the front page of *Le Clairon du Soir*. You're so proud of your hair."

The journalist laughed and embraced his daughter. They walked out of the room arm in arm. The cat meowed angrily and turned its back.

And so while at one end of Paris Koko and Zlatko were walking along Avenue Gambetta toward the barbershop, on the other end, not far from the Bois de Boulogne, Marie Cléver and her father were walking along Rue d'Auteuil in the direction of Place d'Auteuil, where the journalist had spotted a new barbershop that morning. No one could have guessed that anything linked those two pairs—the two boys from Zagreb and the two Parisians—or the two barbers who owned the shops—but the stream of events was bringing them closer together by the minute.

Marie Cléver paused in the middle of the street, looked at her father with her bright eyes, and asked bluntly, "Worson tossed you out, didn't he? Didn't he? No talks, no interviews, no big article. That's why you're running away." The cars were honking furiously.

"But, Marie!" The journalist was astonished by this outburst. He pulled his daughter over to the sidewalk.

"No 'but,' Father. Would you voluntarily retire to

the country, into a mousehole, now that a film is being made about the *Mona Lisa* and after writing that splendid article?"

"So, you've read it already, Marie? You read much too much. That's bad."

"Your not telling me the truth is what's bad. Will you really sit somewhere out in the country while Worson's making that movie, will you?"

"I've got to rest, Marie, I'm telling you."

"And you told your paper you wouldn't write any more articles about the *Mona Lisa?*"

"I haven't told them anything, Marie. I don't *have* to tell them anything. I'm their top reporter, and if I don't feel like writing for a month, I don't have to. They know I'm working on a surprise story."

"Darn it," said Marie, and she stamped her foot on the pavement. The cars were honking because she had again stopped in the middle of the street. "So, that's it, Papa. You're preparing a surprise story, but you're not telling me about it. Well, have it your way, but don't expect me to tell you anything, or to confide in you ever again."

"But, Marie, wait!"

It was too late. The girl said a quick good-bye to her father and, flying between automobiles, ran across the street in the direction of Boulevard de Montmorency. The journalist followed his daughter with his eyes for a while, then smiled and walked across the street and into the barbershop, which had a sign in large gold letters: FRÉDÉRIC'S.

"Good afternoon," said Marcel Cléver on entering the shop.

"Good afternoon, sir," replied the barber, rising from his chair and putting the paper aside. "What will it be, sir?"

"A haircut and a shave."

As he was sitting down, the journalist stole a glance at the barber—a tall, slightly stooped man, with a long and untidy moustache fluttering under his nose—and at the newspapers in the shop. He saw *Le Monde, Figaro,* and *France Soir* lying around.

Marcel Cléver squirmed discontentedly in his chair. An untidy moustache is not a particularly good recommendation for a barber; to make matters worse, the barber evidently didn't carry *Le Clairon du Soir*. Cléver divided people into those who read *Le Clairon du Soir* and those who didn't.

"You don't read *Le Clairon du Soir?*"

"I beg your pardon?" asked the barber, awkwardly tying the towel around the journalist's neck.

"You yourself may not read *Le Clairon du Soir,* but you should have it on the premises for your customers. It's the most widely read paper in Paris today."

"Of course, sir. I must get it. The next time you come here you'll have it, sir."

The journalist gave him an angry look and asked,

"You just opened this shop, didn't you?"

"Yes, sir, two days ago."

"Ouch," the journalist yelled as the clumsy barber poked his ear with the point of his sharp scissors. "I won't ask any more questions. I don't want to distract you."

But sitting still didn't help poor Marcel Cléver. The barber flailed his scissors in the air as if reaping grain, and soon hair was flying all over the place. But if the haircut was frightful, the shave was truly horrendous.

First, the barber soaped the journalist's face—all the way up to his forehead, including his nostrils and eyes, so that the poor man could neither see nor breathe. Then, clutching the razor like a saber, he began to scrape mercilessly.

When Frédéric finally washed his face, the bewildered journalist caught sight in the mirror of a head that bore no resemblance to his own. His hair lay every which way, and his cheeks and neck were bloody. He had rehearsed a number of blistering comments to make to the barber, but when the job was done, he was so relieved to be alive that he ran out of the shop without a word.

"This man is a butcher, not a barber. Infamous! Good God, I haven't paid him! But he didn't ask anything. Strange! I've never experienced anything like this in my life. He'll never see me again, that's for sure. Marie would have had a good laugh if she'd been with me."

And while strollers on Rue d'Auteuil gazed in astonishment at the hysterical and ravaged journalist, Frédéric

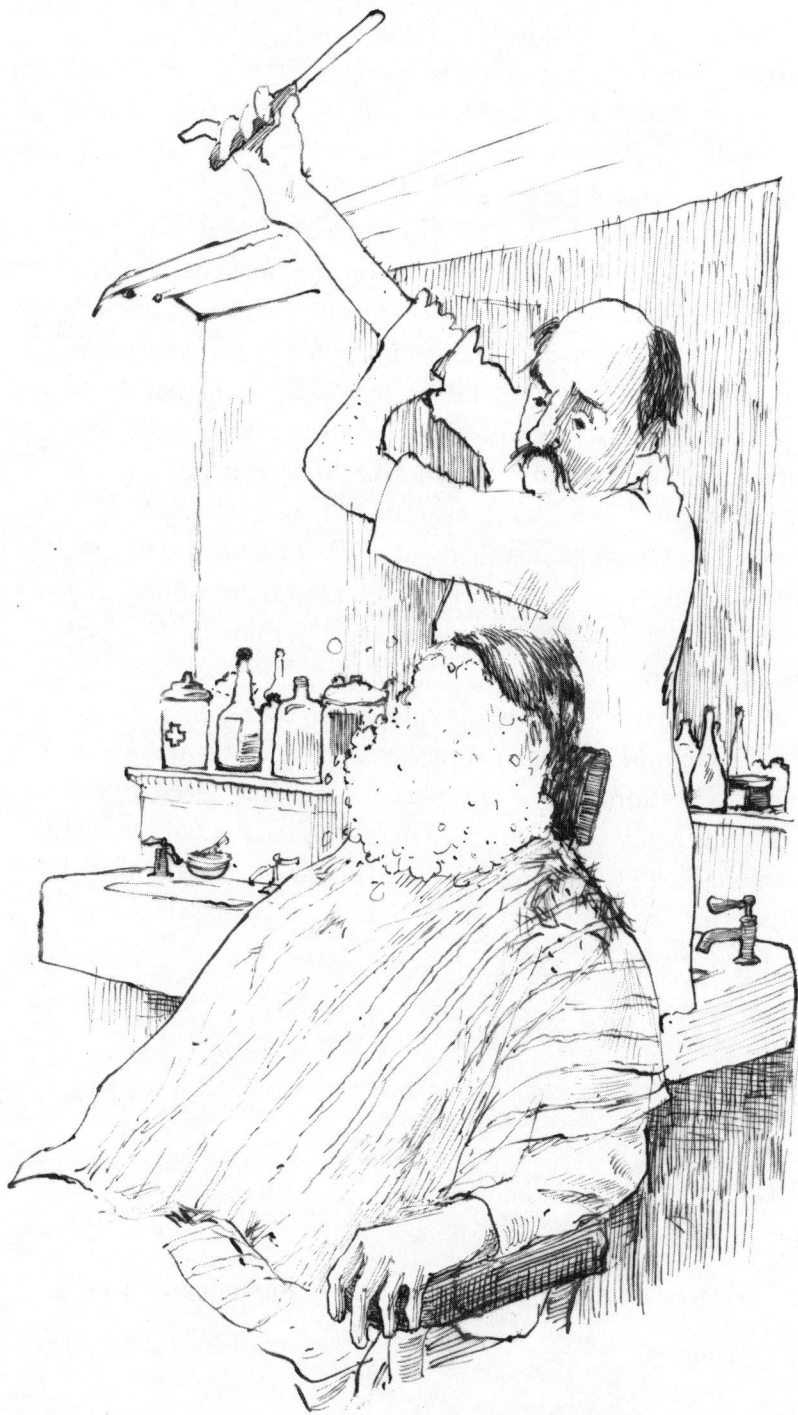

the barber was in an even more wretched condition. Worn out and dripping with sweat, he had collapsed into a chair. Now, mopping the sweat from his brow, he picked up the phone.

He dialed and said in a crushed voice, "Charles, is that you? Charles, I can't go on with this masquerade any longer. This is ridiculous. I'll end up cutting someone's throat, or someone'll end up killing me. And, of course, it goes without saying, I'll be reported to the police. If you could only see what I've just done to a man. His own mother wouldn't recognize him. He ran out of here like it was a slaughterhouse. I forgot to ask him to pay. No, Charles, I can't go on. What did you say? Are you telling me not to rave? Easier said than done, my friend. I'm locking up the shop this minute. I'm not staying here. Not me."

A moment later the distraught Frédéric had locked the shop and was sprinting toward the Porte d'Auteuil Métro station. Three-quarters of an hour later, as we already know, he would burst into Charles's barbershop where Koko's suffering had already come to an end and Zlatko's was only beginning.

"Hands up!" We've got you!

8 By the time Koko was madly rushing down from the balcony of the house on Rue Bretonneau, he had forgotten the barber Charles and his curious guest Frédéric. One might even say that he had forgotten where he was or where he was going. His head didn't clear until he reached Place Paul-Signac, where he continued to run along Avenue Gambetta in pursuit of the mysterious red car.

"Zlatko thinks I'm crazy," Koko thought as he ran under the long rows of trees along Avenue Gambetta. "Let him. But he's in for a surprise!"

Koko Milich was thirteen years old, which by comparison with the Caucasian mountain people who live to be a hundred and fifty or so, is not particularly old. And yet this boy, with a pointed nose and shaggy hair, seemingly very much like his contemporaries, had experienced more within the last few years than most people do in a lifetime. In the village of Green Hill where he had grown up, he had set traps for thieves, and when his family moved to the city, he had fought ghosts and solved the mystery of a boy who had two names and attended two different schools. He had fallen off a roof and almost died in a boat caught in the middle of a whirling river. But he had never yet run aimlessly along a street in a strange city, not knowing where he was going. In the past, when he was seized by fear and a desire to run, he had always been spurred on by the thought of how much his friends would admire him if he behaved cleverly and boldly and how they would tease him if he behaved like a coward. So he kept going.

"Zlatko thinks I'm imagining things, having hallucinations. Let him! I know what I know," he thought time and again.

So Koko never noticed that he had run past the barbershop in which he had been so ill treated earlier that day. Nor did he notice that he had passed Place Gambetta and was heading west, beyond the miniscule part of Paris he had gotten to know since his arrival.

"I understand it all," he kept repeating. "I understand. I understood right off. I just didn't dare tell Zlatko. Why did his uncle lock the attic with four padlocks but never bother with the balcony door? Anyone could get in through the balcony door and make off with the painting, and that's exactly what happened. When I climbed up into the attic, they were probably on their way out with it. They must have heard me, they got scared, and while I was arguing down there with that stubborn mule Zlatko, they put the painting back behind the screen. By the time I got back up onto the balcony, they had already hopped into their car."

A red car. How could he have forgotten the red car? After all, he had rushed out into the street in the hopes of seeing which way the thieves were going.

The boy stood in the middle of a strange square, scratching behind his ear. In the middle of the square, behind an iron fence, rose the monument of a large woman in a wrinkled dress. Koko was thinking of the awful position he was in, and he was very upset. Suddenly he became aware of noise and thick traffic, of streams of automobiles whirling around the monument and flowing into side streets. Many of the cars were red, too. Every minute at least ten red cars sped by the disappointed boy.

"The cripple," Koko thought bitterly. "How could I have forgotten the cripple? That character must be the leader of the thieves. With his crippled leg he couldn't possibly have run that fast. I must have run right past him—probably hiding in some bar or other. I am really a fool."

In despair, the boy crossed the Place de la République and then followed a great big boulevard into the huge commotion of Paris at dusk. Flashing neon lights began to appear, particularly on the marquees of the many movie houses on Boulevard St.-Martin. Slowly darkness was enveloping Paris.

Koko was not thinking of the possibilities of danger

"Hands up! We've got you!" [69]

until, crossing the street, he bumped into a modestly dressed man carrying an armful of flowers and offering them for sale. Suddenly Zlatko's words echoed in his brain: "Some beggar or other passes by, for example, and offers you flowers for sale. You sniff the flowers and faint." In an attempt to avoid the flower vendor, the boy bumped into a blindman who raised his white cane in defense. "He'll shoot," Koko thought feverishly and began to run.

Then, to his great consternation, he realized that he was lost. Perhaps the thieves had planned this whole game to get him into the depths of Paris where they could seize him. Koko paused. A bead of perspiration slid down his nose and dripped onto his chin.

"Take it easy, Koko." He tried to buck himself up. "You'll go back home and tell your sister and Tom and Boza about how you were being chased by cripples with trained parrots and red cars, but that you wouldn't let them confuse you or scare you."

Koko, afraid of giving himself away, did not dare to ask for directions. At the next intersection he took a left turn, hoping that would take him back to Avenue Gambetta and the Pelleport Métro station.

"I'm a fool," he kept saying to himself, trying to dispel black thoughts and never quite admitting to himself that he might have gotten lost in Paris. "I'm a fool not to have looked in the doorways along Rue Bretonneau. What a fool I am! I'll bet that cripple is laughing his head off. And Zlatko? What will Zlatko say? He'll tease the life out of me when I see him again . . ."

"When I see him again!" The thought that it might be a long time before he saw Zlatko again was terrifying. Now he wouldn't mind Zlatko's teasing him, or scrubbing his back under a cold shower for that matter, just so he could catch sight of his square, hard, dear old head.

Where could Zlatko be now? Was he discussing Koko's disappearance with his uncle? Had he informed the police? Or was he out looking for him all over the city? Koko felt that he had been walking not for hours but for days and that he would soon collapse from fatigue and hunger. Yes, from hunger! The last food he had was candy on the plane, and that was hours ago.

"Surely he'll find me. He must find me. Paris isn't that big. Of course, I could ask someone for the way. Why not? I know the address, the telephone number. They can't all be the cripple's agents. Surely I have nothing to be afraid of."

It was almost dark. Koko was turning left, and left again, convinced that he was slowly turning toward Zlatko's uncle's apartment, when suddenly he found himself on a bridge over the Seine. The old-fashioned orange lamps on the stone bridge were reflected in the deep green river, along which white illuminated boats glided. But Koko couldn't concentrate on the boats. He crossed the bridge and turned left again.

He finally spotted a familiar place and almost

screamed with delight. "Notre Dame!" said Koko aloud, and he looked around for fear someone might have overheard him.

For a moment he thought he was back in his little room on Buzanova Street in Zagreb, quietly leafing through the Paris guidebooks. In those days, he had looked forward to his trip to the big city, never suspecting what lay ahead.

With a leisurely step Koko approached Notre Dame. The magnificent structure, illuminated on all sides by concealed spotlights and standing out in stark contrast to the black sky, looked more mysterious than any fairy-tale castle. If he hadn't been so tired, Koko would have enjoyed this beautiful building more than any zoo with seventy whales.

For some time Koko walked back and forth in front of Notre Dame. He wanted to go inside, but changed his mind when he recalled Zlatko's stories about the Notre Dame hunchbacks who attacked their innocent victims at night.

Finally, he sauntered off to a quiet open space by the side of the church and sat down on a grassy spot not far from a monument of a bold man on a great horse. He stared at the brilliantly illuminated building, and suddenly the steeples began to dance before his eyes and the figures of strange winged animals with which the church was bedecked came to life and began to stir, crawl, fly. Koko's eyes were smarting; his eyelids grew as

heavy as if they, too, were made of stone. He thought he was dreaming or that he might faint.

"Zlatko, where are you now?" he wondered, feeling that he would burst into tears. "Where are you now, Zlatko? You brought me here to Paris. It was your idea. You must get me out of this."

At that instant powerful bony fingers tightened around his neck, and he heard a piercing voice in back of him.

"Hands up! We've got you!"

Complex as cobwebs

9 César, the parrot, jumped in fright at the sound of a piercing whistle from the street outside. First three whistles, and then three more.

Katsarida was quietly sitting in a huge armchair, reading a magazine. From time to time he would look out over the Bois de Boulogne and think how wonderful it would be to ride a bicycle in the park and race with his friends. He'd be the fastest, and some day, very soon, he'd become as famous as the great cyclist Anquetil.

"That's Marie," the boy cried happily when he heard the whistling. He leaped up from the armchair, sending a lapful of magazines tumbling onto the floor. "What a whistle! Good thing my father isn't home or he'd be shouting at the top of his lungs. If only he knew who's doing the whistling!"

"Crack!" said César, straightening out with his beak his fear-ruffled feathers.

Katsarida quickly opened the door, almost knocking

over Maurice who was on his way to remind the boy to practice the piano. Quick as a flash Katsarida darted out of the house.

On the other side of Boulevard de Montmorency, under the plane trees, Marie Cléver was waiting for him impatiently.

"You're a slowpoke," she said and shook her head.

"I got here as fast as I could," Katsarida apologized. "You know how it is in our household. Anyway, I have something important to tell you."

"I know," the girl said indifferently. "That's why I'm here. You don't think I came to see you, Katsar, do you? We can't talk in the street, though, can we? I'm not supposed to go into your house, right? I'm not afraid, of course, but you are. What would your dear father say? He'd spank you with his cane, I'll bet."

"Marie, don't talk that way. You know I'm not afraid. If you want to. . . . My father isn't home."

"See?" Marie was gleeful. "Your father isn't home. You *are* afraid! If he were there, you wouldn't dare invite me in, right? 'Miss Cléver,' your old butler said on the phone yesterday, 'it would be better for you not to call the young master because it makes Mr. Somais angry. Besides, the young master is practicing right now.' "

"Marie, don't tease me. It's not my fault." The boy defended himself, lowering his head in embarrassment.

"Aren't you embarrassed to be playing the piano, Katsar, in this day and age? The twentieth century?

You love bicycles and sports, and here you are pounding away at the piano all day. You should be ashamed of yourself. You should play the guitar. That's just in case someone asks you."

"I'd love to play the guitar. I've told my father a hundred times . . ."

The girl made a contemptuous gesture, as if to dismiss the whole subject, and started to cross the street. Katsarida had no choice but to follow her, although he had no idea where she was going.

"Some day I'll be a famous bicyclist," the boy thought bitterly as he followed her sheepishly. "I'll win the Tour de France three times in a row, and I'll play the guitar better than anyone else in the world. Then she'll be sorry. She'll treat me differently, but it'll be too late."

Marie Cléver paused and said resolutely, "Since you don't seem to have any ideas, I guess I'll have to do all the thinking. You act as if you've never read a spy story in your life. We'll get into your garden through the back door and hide in the arbor. No one will know we're there, and we can talk quietly."

Katsarida had to admit to himself that Marie was able to think faster than he could. They could have simply walked into the Bois de Boulogne and sat down on the first bench they came across, but it was much more fun to pretend that the safest and the quietest place in the whole wide world for a confidential talk was the shady arbor in the back of Somais's large garden.

When they finally found themselves in the green twilight behind the thick wall of the ivy, Marie Cléver sat down in a wicker chair, then quickly stood up and pushed the surprised boy into it.

"Speak!" she said, in the tone of a prosecuting attorney. "Tell me why you asked me to come here!"

"I mean," the boy stammered, rolling his green eyes, "I thought if your father, I mean . . ."

"My father has disappeared," the girl cut in. "Don't ask me why or how. It's enough for me to say we can't count on my father. He's being very difficult. He's obviously got something on his mind."

"Ah," Katsarida interrupted. "That's what I thought. He must be suspicious."

"Suspicious of what? Look, Katsarida, take hold of yourself. Think before you speak. Why did you ask me to come here if you haven't got something to tell me?"

"The *Mona Lisa*." The boy finally got it off his chest and sighed.

"The *Mona Lisa!*" Marie stamped the ground hard. "That's what I thought! *That*'s why my father's been so mysterious."

"My father'll soon be launching a big new transatlantic ship, the biggest in his fleet."

"So what? What has that got to do with the *Mona Lisa*? You should read my father's article in *Le Clairon du Soir*. About the movie being made at the Louvre. About the *Mona Lisa* and the man who stole it."

Marie Cléver told the boy the story in great detail, including the episode in which the thief's friend suspects that the "fake" is in fact the original, and the thief ties his friend to a chair, right smack under the picture, where he would have died of hunger if a beautiful girl hadn't come to his rescue. But Katsarida was not interested in the movie. What interested him was how the guards would protect the painting at the Louvre during the filming.

"Did you say they'd do the shooting with the fake?" Katsarida asked.

"Yes, but the fake resembles the original so closely that the painter himself can hardly tell the difference. It's amazing!"

"Ah, well." The boy was on his feet again. "That's enough for my father. Nothing in the world will stop him from trying to get the painting. He'll do anything and pay vast sums of money. Oh, Marie, it really frightens me."

"Coward!" the girl cried and stamped with her foot again. "If you're frightened, you shouldn't have asked me to come here in the first place, right?"

"My father'll have the fake hanging on the wall of the Louvre after the filming, and the original will be on his new ship. That's what happened when. . . . Well, when it comes to the great masters, my father isn't quite sane. Perhaps it's because he wanted to be a painter himself. The same thing happened with the *Cleopatra.*"

"*Cleopatra!*" the girl screamed. "So that's it! Now I understand! Why didn't you tell me this right away?"

Marie Cléver had sorted it out instantly in her intelligent little head. At least so it seemed to her. She remembered the *Cleopatra* affair vividly, when the famous Raphael painting disappeared from the Louvre two years ago. The trouble began when the painting of the dark-haired Egyptian queen was sent to the restorers for work. The painting that came back to the Louvre, it was discovered, was not the original. Marcel Cléver of *Le Clairon du Soir* made quite a name for himself in this whole matter. He pointed out that no one could sell the painting to a reputable dealer or collector or museum— no one could publicly display a stolen property—it must have been bought by a very rich eccentric who kept it under lock and key in some place where he could admire it secretly. "Shipowners are among the richest people in the world," Cléver wrote, "and many collect art. Perhaps it is in this group that we should look for Raphael's masterpiece."

"It was around that time that Father commissioned his new transatlantic liner *Cleopatra*," Katsarida added, looking around carefully. "I sailed on its maiden voyage from New York to Greece. My father was in a great state of nerves. His leg hurt. I heard him complaining about a Paris journalist who had accused him of having stolen Raphael's *Cleopatra*. The basis for the accusation was that my father had named his new ship *Cleopatra*. And then one night, when I came out on the deck . . ."

"What happened?" Marie asked, her eyes sparkling with curiosity.

"I had noticed," the boy continued, "that every night my father would go into a tiny cabin under the bridge and lock himself in. The next day I came across a copy of *Le Clairon du Soir* in his cabin, and it all became quite clear. Every evening my father would lock himself in, and every day he grew increasingly irritable, drank a lot, and suffered this great pain in his leg."

"And then what happened?" the girl asked, and then completed the story herself. "After you reached Greece, the *Cleopatra* was found in the port of Piraeus in a barrel, right?"

"When we got back to Paris, suddenly, like a bolt from the blue, he heard on the radio that a drunk had found the painting in Piraeus. My father finally calmed down, stopped drinking, his leg no longer hurt. Toward the end there he had felt so threatened that he couldn't wait to get rid of the picture."

"Do you think that now," Marie whispered, "that now, with the *Mona Lisa* . . ."

The girl didn't dare complete the sentence, and the boy didn't dare elaborate, but merely nodded. In the twilight of the arbor a pair of green eyes stared at a pair of gray eyes. It was as if a big cobweb had been spun between Marie Cléver and Katsarida that they didn't dare touch. The boy and the girl had no idea what to do with the great secret the two had woven.

"Bravo, Katsar, you are fantastic!" Marie said and put her hand gently on the boy's dark head.

"Oh," gasped the Greek in embarrassment.

"We've got to do something right away," Marie went on, thinking of Mata Hari, who would surely have known by now exactly what course of action to take.

"We've got to do something right away," echoed Katsarida as his face turned almost yellow with fear.

The devil's advice

IO Frédéric Brange and Charles Croitier both had teen-age sons, one named Jean and the other Michel. The two boys were inseparable friends, even though they were five years apart in age. Jean was eighteen. He had just graduated from high school. Michel was only thirteen. Their parents found it rather curious that, in spite of their age difference, the two boys should be such close friends. It was funny to see them together in the street. Jean was tall, two heads taller than Michel, and sported a little moustache. He also smoked. Michel had silky dark hair, slanting eyes, and pronounced cheekbones. He was always trotting along next to Jean, desperately trying to keep up with the latter's long strides.

When there was cause for unhappiness, they were both sad, and when there was cause for happiness, they both celebrated. They didn't live together, and yet they awoke in the same mood every morning. If Jean got up on the wrong foot, so would Michel, and if Michel whistled in his house while getting ready for school, one could be sure that Jean would be humming as he brushed his teeth.

They were different in only one respect. Jean had a driver's license, and after graduation his uncle had given him a car. True enough, it was an ancient little Citroën, which shook as if it were going to fall apart any minute. Even so, it rolled at quite a decent speed, and the boys were enormously proud of it. It was hard to tell which one of them was more proud: Jean, the true owner, or Michel, who would rather ride in that Citroën than in any Rolls Royce.

Today was one of those days when both Jean and Michel were unhappy.

"Michel," said Jean when they met that afternoon in front of the Louvre. "I'm fed up."

"Jean," said Michel, "I feel ghastly."

Some time earlier Mr. Croitier had promised to take his son Michel to the coast as soon as he had seen his report card, and Mr. Brange had promised his son Jean they'd get into the Citroën for a drive along the river Loire to see all those magical castles. The boys kept their end of the bargain. Their grades were excellent, but the fathers did not keep up their end. Both had to stay in Paris on important business. The trips to the Riviera and to the Loire would have to wait. The mothers couldn't be of much assistance. Frédéric Brange and Charles Croitier were very stubborn men.

Today Michel and Jean learned that it was not merely

a postponement of their departure, but that there was a chance that they wouldn't leave Paris that summer at all.

"Father," Jean had asked, "do you mean to say that we may not go *anywhere* this summer?"

"Not at all," his father replied. "You and your mother may visit your grandmother in the country, or your aunt in Lyon, any time you wish."

"Father," Jean replied, "this will not end well." He walked toward the door.

"What will not end well?" Frédéric Brange asked in alarm. He gave his wife a desperate look and rolled his eyes. "What could you possibly mean, Jean, when you say . . ."

But Frédéric didn't get a chance to finish his sentence. Jean had banged the door so hard that the large wall clock let out a little cry and then stopped altogether.

At the same time, at the other end of Paris, Michel had asked the same question and received a similar reply from his father.

So it was that when Jean and Michel met in front of the Louvre a little while later, there was no end to their disappointment and bitterness. They piled into the old Citroën and cruised aimlessly in the famous late-afternoon Paris traffic crush in which pedestrians move faster than automobiles.

"If only I had even a clue of a clue," said Jean, "why they have to stay in town in this heat. I don't understand my mother. Why doesn't she do something?"

"Ah, well," Michel said philosophically, "it must be some special job again. If only I could find out what it is."

"I don't understand them," said Jean. "They must need vacations. People aren't machines. But the two don't seem to know what it is to rest."

Michel was very upset. "The work they do! Some work. It's a shame!"

"Listen," Jean said, suddenly terribly grave. He almost slammed into the car in front of them. "Do you think, Michel, it's something fishy again? You think they may be involved again?"

"They're up to something," Michel replied, his eyes moist with anguish. "They'll get caught up in some crazy game, like last year when they played firemen and my old man fell down the chimney."

"Or the year before last, when they repaired that millionaire's plumbing and opened a gas valve instead of the water and almost suffocated," recalled Jean.

"Or when. . . . " Michel began again, but he burst into such laughter that the tears welled into his eyes. He simply couldn't regain his breath.

"They think nothing of impersonating toreadors or barbers or doctors. You name it—they've done it."

"Ha, ha," Michel said with a laugh, still clutching his stomach. "Wouldn't they be great as barbers? I'd love to see that! My old man is so awkward that he'd cut the throat of his first customer, ha, ha."

"It might even pay that way," Jean said seriously.

"Who knows how much money barbers make?"

"Not very much, I'll bet. To make really big money, you have to rob a bank. Hey, where're you going?"

Jean had spotted a tiny parking space in front of Notre Dame. He made a large circular turn and wedged the small Citroën between two big cars. The boys stepped out of the car and headed for the nearest café for a Coke.

Jean lit a cigarette and said, "We should think of some way of making sure they remember the summer they left us in Paris."

"Right!" Michel said and smiled defiantly. "But how?"

Michel and Jean had been sitting for some time at a small table in a café on Rue d'Arcole, sipping their drinks. They were thinking very hard about what kind of adventure they could set in motion, something that would divert their parents from their own curious pre-occupations and make them concentrate on the two boys, Jean and Michel, who had done so very well in school but would not, even so, get to see the castles of the Loire or the Riviera. They didn't think it was so easy to rob a bank, but that was very much on their minds; they felt that only a really dangerous prank would make an impression on their fathers.

"How about robbing a bank anyway?" Michel repeated. "What do you say?"

"Why not kidnap somebody's kid? That would be something, wouldn't it? Remember the Peugeot kid-

napping? All of Paris was stirred up. Just take a look around you and you're sure to find a good victim. Foreigners aren't bad at all. Their fathers may be rich, millionaires, and if you telephone them and demand a large ransom, you'll at least get into the newspapers, right? That's what you're after, isn't it? Much simpler than robbing a bank. I'll bet you that if you look around the cathedral right now, you'll find some kid wandering around who may be lost for all you know. You stuff him into your car—one, two, three—you find a tele-

phone, you dial the father's number, you tell him what's what . . ."

Jean and Michel were so astonished that they almost fell under the table. They couldn't believe their ears. But once they had recovered from the shock, they looked around to see who in the world would dare give them such advice. At the next table sat an unusual-looking man drinking a glass of beer and smiling pleasantly. Over his right eye was a large black patch, and his left leg was wooden.

The devil's advice [89]

"We don't know you, sir," said Jean.

"But I know you, and that's all that matters, wouldn't you agree?" said the cripple and smiled again. "And I know what your problem is. The ransom part may never come off, but the kidnapping will. The two of you should have no trouble overcoming a thin little boy . . ."

"Good-bye, sir," Jean said with determination. He jumped up and started down the street, with Michel keeping pace beside him.

"I'll take care of your check, as you seem to have forgotten it. Don't bother to come back," the cripple called after them. "You'd better hurry, or that bird'll fly away now, won't it?"

Jean blushed, paused for a moment, waved, and then continued to walk away. He felt uncomfortable about going back. He was afraid to have any more dealings with the mysterious cripple.

"Let him pay if he wants to," he said.

"Sure," said Michel, and hopping on the tips of his toes to get as close as he could to Jean's ear, he whispered, "Are we really going to grab a kid?"

"Michel, you're out of your mind," Jean snapped and felt cold. "You are . . ."

He never completed his sentence. They crossed the street and passed in front of the great façade of Notre Dame. Michel caught up with Jean and grabbed his sleeve, pointing with his nose in the direction of Charlemagne. Jean and Michel froze on the spot. They saw a boy with unruly hair, thin legs, and pointed nose, scratching himself behind the ear. Jean and Michel, the two Parisians, saw Ratko Milich, nicknamed Koko, for the first time in their lives.

You can't be too careful

II Poklé stroked his beard with great satisfaction and finally rose from the floor. He had been kneeling in front of the *Mona Lisa* for a full ten minutes. He had sent the boys off to get haircuts so he could enjoy the famous artwork all by himself. He had been going through similar rituals for several days now. At first he couldn't wait to bring someone up to his messy little flat on Rue Bretonneau to show off the treasure, but then he would want to be alone with it and undisturbed.

"The boys are charming," the painter thought, "but they have no idea what the *Mona Lisa* is and what it means to paint a copy of it so well that not even the experts can tell the difference. I've been looking at it long enough, though. I've got to get a breath of fresh air."

He lowered the three curtains, locked the four padlocks, and hid the four keys. Finally he lit his pipe—he didn't dare smoke up there in front of the painting—and left his apartment.

"When I get rich," the painter thought, "I'll buy a country house outside Paris and a large studio with skylights and big windows, and I will paint the sun, blue suns. . . . And as for tobacco, I'll never again smoke this cheap stuff, only the best. Oh, my pipe's out again."

He had reached the Place Paul-Signac—a square named after the famous French painter, which is why Poklé loved to sit in one of its cafés and drink wine. His pipe had gone out, and he had run out of matches. While he was nervously rummaging through his pockets, a cripple with a wooden leg and a black patch on his left eye approached.

"Can I give you a light, sir?" the cripple asked and smiled affably.

"Oh, thank you very much. I seem to be out of matches."

The cripple gave him a book of matches, and the painter, having lit his pipe, absentmindedly shoved them into his pocket. He was about to go, but the cripple gently touched his sleeve.

"Would you mind having a glass of wine with me?"

"Very kind of you, indeed," the painter said, somewhat baffled, "but I don't have the time. I mean, I have the time, but I'm tired and would like to take a little stroll."

"I understand. Well, another time perhaps. One never knows when one might have an interesting time. See you again, Mr. Poklé."

It wasn't until Poklé had crossed the street that he

realized how odd it was that this stranger knew his name. But before he was able to think when and where they might have met, the cripple had yelled after him, "If you want to get a shave or a haircut, I'd recommend the new barbershop at the end of Avenue Gambetta. It's called CHARLES'S."

More confused now than before, Poklé accelerated his step without looking back—and in his confusion walked in the wrong direction. At the second intersection he turned right and walked downtown. Puffing on his pipe, he concluded half in jest: "Perhaps my name is known in Paris, perhaps Paris knows me. . . . Ah, but this is only a taste of things of come."

His mind wandered from one thought to another. He recalled that he had forgotten to feed the two boys that day. At that point he suddenly paused in front of a barbershop with a large, sparkling sign announcing CHARLES'S. Yes, that was the barbershop to which he had sent Zlatko and Koko and which the strange cripple had recommended to him. He grabbed the hair on the nape of his neck, passed his hand under his beard, and decided that perhaps he should get a shave. "Now I'll have to take better care of myself," he thought with satisfaction. "I can no longer walk around Paris unshaved. I'm not just anybody now. . . ."

When he entered the barbershop, the very place from which Zlatko and Koko had emerged somewhat the worse for wear sometime before, it was empty. At the other end, behind the curtain, he heard voices. Poklé

You can't be too careful [95]

walked over to the curtain and overheard two men talking frantically. "I think we ought to feed him."

"Not now. We've got more important things to do."

"Listen, Charles, you don't want anything to happen to him . . ."

"But what do you feed him? You don't know what he's used to."

"Frédéric, if something happens to him . . ."

The painter thought to himself angrily, "I should have fed the boys. After the shave I'll go straight home and prepare a steak and potatoes for them."

To lure the barber out from behind the curtain, the painter coughed loudly. The moustached head of Frédéric Brange appeared, and instead of greeting the painter, Frédéric asked him, as if it were the most natural question in the world and as if it were the only way to greet new customers, "Excuse me, sir, but do you know what parrots eat?"

Poklé was so amazed by the question that some smoke got caught in his windpipe. Before he was able to reply, Frédéric turned green and withdrew behind the curtain. He put his hand on Charles's shoulder and said almost inaudibly, "That's him . . . him. He . . . he's here. I mean it . . ."

Charles stuck his wide nose out through the opening between the curtains and pulled it right back in again.

"You're right, Frédéric. That's him! Frédéric, let's get to work."

"Right away? Right away, Charles?"

"Of course. This is what we've been waiting for."

"And we'll keep him here as long as we can."

"Of course. Don't worry."

"Mind you don't cut his throat."

"Frédéric!"

The two barbers finally emerged from behind the curtain. They bowed deeply and shook hands with the painter as if they were old friends. In a split second he was put into the chair. He just barely had time to put his pipe down. Charles quickly wrapped him in white towels from head to foot, tying one around his neck so tight that the painter gasped, "Hemp, I think . . . hemp seeds."

"Yes, of course," replied Charles, forgetting that he had asked the painter a while back what to feed his parrot. "I understand, sir. A haircut and a shave."

Frédéric dawdled a while longer. Charles gave him a filthy look. He bowed again to the painter, or rather to the small portion of the painter that peered and poked through all those towels, and left the shop like a shot.

"Ow! Please be careful!" Poklé yelled. The barber had accidentally stuck an elbow into Poklé's left eye. Little did Poklé suspect, the poor man, that his tortures were only beginning.

"Do you like it high or low?" asked the barber with an enigmatic smile.

"Hemp," replied the bewildered painter, wondering

how he had ended up in the barber's chair. As a rule it took him months to make up his mind to cross the threshold of that torture chamber.

But Charles wasn't listening to him anyway, so it didn't really matter what he said. Charles was concerned about one thing: to keep his visitor in that chair as long as possible. He took a very long time sharpening that razor. He looked endlessly for the right kind of scissors. And when he finally got to work on the painter's head, he started snipping off tiny bits of hair, one by one.

He was at it for over an hour. From the back, the painter resembled a sick hen. The barber showed no signs of ever completing the job, certainly not until the last thin little hair on that head was cut.

"I think that should do it," said the painter in a feeble voice at the end of his second hour of suffering in that chair.

"And a shave, sir, did you say?" Charles cheerfully began sharpening his razor again.

"Those two boys will die of hunger, like parrots," the painter thought dismally, suddenly terribly depressed. His heart was full of gruesome forebodings. His eyes accidentally paused on a calendar that was hanging on the wall. He realized for the first time that it was Friday.

"Good God!" he whimpered. With the first bold move of the razor, the barber cut him right behind the ear.

"You shouldn't squirm," Charles said. "You're like a child. If you don't sit still, I'll end up cutting your throat."

The poor painter rolled his eyes and kept as still as possible. The most important thing was to stay alive and to make an escape from this butcher at the first possible moment.

Among the sharks in the lake

12 "Shall we?" asked Michel once again, but with more determination this time around.

Jean's bright eyes glowed in the spotlights illuminating Notre Dame. He would have stalled a little longer if he hadn't suddenly remembered the Loire and all the marvelous castles he wouldn't see this summer.

"How about it?" Michel was persistent. He was thinking about the Mediterranean he wouldn't see. "Why not do something preposterous here in Paris?"

"Let's!" Jean said suddenly.

Meanwhile, tired and hungry, Koko was staring dully at the illuminated cathedral and thinking about how his friend Zlatko would surely be able to find him in the big city.

Jean and Michel opened the back door of their Citroën, tiptoed around the boy who was sitting on the turf, and hid themselves in the shrubbery at the base of the monument, impatiently awaiting the right time. The moment there was no one in sight, they pounced.

Jean grabbed Koko by the neck with his bony fingers and yelled the first thing that came to mind, or what he thought should be yelled in this situation: "Hands up! We've got you!"

In the twinkling of an eye they tied a handkerchief over his mouth and pushed him through the back door of the little Citroën. Michel got in next to Koko; Jean took the wheel. The car quickly merged with the night bustle of Paris.

Koko felt as if it were all a terrible nightmare from which he might awake at any moment.

They raced through the streets of Paris at such speed that Koko covered his eyes. He was sure they'd have an accident. Michel suddenly removed the handkerchief from Koko's mouth and asked cheerfully, "Well, old man, how are you? Scared stiff?"

"No, I'm not scared," Koko replied, somewhat surprised at the sound of his own voice. For one thing, it showed courage that he had even opened his mouth, and just as much courage that he had understood and spoken French. All those irregular verbs and adjectives were strewn across his mind like the parts of a broken clock, but now, at the crucial moment, the whole machinery was assembled and keeping remarkably good time. Koko speaking French! If only Zlatko could hear him now!

"A foreigner, eh?" Jean asked, glancing back.

"Yes," Koko replied.

"Are your parents rich?" Jean continued, turning

toward the boy. Koko looked at him with curiosity: thick eyebrows, bright eyes, and a suggestion of a moustache. He could have sworn he had seen him somewhere before.

"No, my parents are not rich."

"Did you hear that, Michel? A terrible waste."

"Listen, old boy." Michel addressed Koko in a voice full of friendship, as if they had known each other for years. "You might say we've been had. What are we going to do with you now?"

"I really don't know. It's not my fault," said Koko, scratching behind the ear.

Michel and Jean laughed.

"We won't let you get away with it that easily," Jean said. "This is our first experience with kidnapping, and we are anxious to have it turn out right. You may not be the son of a rich man, some Peugeot, say, but surely we can think of ways you could be useful to us."

"You've got to help us." Michel encouraged Koko, nudging him in the ribs, his thin eyes narrowed to slits in the semidarkness. "Come on, be a good sport. We've got to think of something. We want to get into the newspapers. But if your old man isn't loaded, there's no point in asking for money."

"I really don't know." Koko tried to explain himself. "I've never been kidnapped before. My sister was kidnapped once, but that was different. Those crooks tried to get us to move out of our apartment."

"In Paris?" Koko looked at him.

"Well, no, I don't live in Paris. We're from Yugoslavia."

"What's your name?" asked Jean.

"Koko."

"An excellent name, old man. What do you say, Jean?"

Jean and Michel introduced themselves formally. By now the three of them were so chummy that if someone had taken a peek at them, he'd never have guessed that this was a clear-cut case of kidnapping—Jean and Michel kidnappers, Koko their victim. The talk was cordial and friendly.

They were now driving through fairly deserted streets, Jean's foot pushing down with increased force. They were obviously some distance from the center of the city. Michel leaned forward and touched the driver's shoulder.

"Where're you taking us, Jean?"

"To Vincennes. To the forest."

"To the forest?" Koko was frightened. "Why to the forest? Isn't this far enough?"

"You're right, Jean. This kind of thing is done in the woods."

"What kind of thing do you mean?" Koko asked gently.

"There are two big forests in Paris, get it, Koko?" Michel explained, his narrow eyes glistening ominously. "The Bois de Boulogne to the west and the Bois de Vincennes to the east. All crimes take place either in one or the other. And the most recent kidnapper—that madman, do you remember, Jean?—he buried his victim in the Bois de Vincennes two months ago. The guy kidnapped the kid, he asked the father for some dough, the father squealed to the police, so the kidnapper . . ."

"I'd like to get out of here," Koko stammered as a bead of perspiration formed on top of his nose. "If you'll let me."

Jean and Michel laughed loudly.

"You don't think we'd actually do you in, do you?" Jean asked through gales of laughter. "We just meant that it was a great place for such things."

"Anyway, now that we've got you, we couldn't let you go just like that. You'd like to get out, you say. You must understand us too. We've been had, haven't we, Jean?"

"You said it," answered Jean as he brought the car to a sudden stop along the tree-lined drive.

"Here we are," said Michel.

Koko timidly peeked out of the window. The skimpy street lights illuminated the road. They were not far from a park that looked like a forest. In the thick greenery one could see the glistening surface of a lake.

"Uaaaa." A horrible scream echoed, and Koko quickly pulled his head back into the Citroën.

"That's the zoo. Don't worry, chum," said Michel.

"We don't have much time"—Jean turned to the two boys in the back seat—"so we'll have to start now. For the time being we won't tie you up, but that doesn't mean that you can get away so fast. On the contrary, if you try, you'll be making a big mistake."

"I won't try anything," Koko cut in.

"We don't know you that well," Jean continued, gathering his thick brows together. "And we don't really know what we can get out of you."

"But you've got to help us, chum, you've simply got to," Michel repeated, placing his arm around Koko's neck in a friendly way. "Just think a little with that ridiculously cropped head of yours. Tell us who to call, who would pay a ransom for you. You must have read about such things in the papers. You won't force us to bury you alive or throw you into the lake with a rock around your neck, like a cat."

"Ouch," Koko gasped. "I'd like to get out of here."

"Don't be ridiculous," Jean said severely. "Kidnapping's a serious matter, and we have no time for joking. We're all in this together, and how well we succeed depends entirely on us. Tell us, Koko, where are you staying in Paris?"

The boy from Yugoslavia described as best he could in French his plane trip, the arrival in Paris, his friend Zlatko and his strange uncle, the painter. Finally he mentioned that the painter had in his attic a very valuable painting, the work of an Italian master from the Stone Age. He then added that he thought the painting was called the *Cleopatra* and that it was the portrait of some actress or other.

"What did you say?" Jean jumped up so hard that he hit the roof of the Citroën. "That must be the precious painting that disappeared once before and that the ship-owner Somais was supposed to have swiped."

"Oh, God," screeched Michel. "And we were wondering what ransom to ask for Koko. That'll be more than enough."

"Of course." Jean opened the car door. "Boys, get out! And no nonsense from you, Koko! Is that clear?"

"Splendid, man, splendid," said Michel cheerfully. "Congratulations. That's great."

As he got out of the car, Koko scratched himself behind the ear. He had no idea what he could have said or done to have made these kidnappers so happy. Besides, one might say, his idea of kidnappers was something altogether different. "They may be just pretending," he thought, "just pretending to be nice, and then suddenly, bang, they'll throw me to the sharks."

Jean nervously lit a cigarette and proposed a plan of action. They would call up the painter, introduce themselves as kidnappers, and ask for the painting. If the uncle refused to deliver the goods or tried to call the police, Koko's goose would be cooked.

"I've got his phone number," Koko confessed sheepishly, uncertain whether that was good or bad.

"Splendid, old man, you're great," said Michel, nudging him in the ribs again.

Jean's plan was now further simplified: first he and Michel would telephone their own families to make sure they didn't raise a stink because their sons hadn't returned home. Michel would say that he was spending the night at Jean's, and Jean would say that he was spending the night at Michel's.

That done, it was Koko's turn.

"You'll tell the painter to take *Cleopatra*—that is, if he wants to see you alive—to get on the subway in the direction of Charenton, and to get off at Porte Dorée station. Our car, the little Citroën, will be waiting for him a hundred yards from the Nautical Museum. He should put the painting down on the sidewalk about ten yards from the car, and one of us will get out with you. We'll pick up the painting, and you can go back into town with him."

Koko understood what was expected of him, and he felt that perhaps there was hope for him and that he might get out of Paris alive after all. All three of them squeezed into the telephone booth; Koko gave the kidnappers the painter's number, and Michel dialed.

Jean jointed his finger at him threateningly and said, "No tricks, you understand!"

The kidnappers listened to a long conversation in a language they didn't understand. Koko spoke fast in a trembling voice, a drop of perspiration suspended from the tip of his pointed nose. He put down the receiver, and they all sighed with relief.

"Well?" Jean asked impatiently.

"Fine. He'll bring the painting," Koko said, looking

proudly at the kidnappers, knowing that without his help they would never get anywhere.

"You're great, chum, just great," Michel said, his eyes moist with pleasure.

"One more thing. I made a mistake," Koko apologized. "It's not *Cleopatra*. It's the *Mona Lisa*."

"What?" Jean was so astonished that he almost choked from the smoke he inhaled the wrong way.

"Ho, ho!" Michel laughed maliciously. "Koko, you're terrific! By tomorrow all Paris will be talking about us, and by the day after tomorrow, the whole wide world, I'm telling you. The papers will say: Two young kidnappers got the most expensive and famous painting in the world. What do you say, Jean? And what will our fathers say? Oh, God!"

Friday, the thirteenth

I3 "I should have fed the boys. They'll die of hunger," the painter concluded as he walked home from the barbershop. He casually paused in front of a shopwindow, catching sight of his own reflection. He was dumbfounded.

"What has that barber done to me?" he said in desperation. "What in heaven's name do I look like now?"

The barber had indeed altered the painter's appearance. There was no trace of the long wavy hair on the nape of his neck. A few isolated tufts of hair stood perched on top of his head like shrubs in the tundra. Most pathetic of all was his beard. The painter's dark beard, streaked with gray here and there, now resembled a well-used toothbrush. Besides, the beard was trimmed at an angle, which made the painter's whole face appear contorted. He noticed that people looked at him with a certain degree of curiosity. He made up his mind that, should he run into the cripple again, he would see to it

that he would need a patch over his left eye as well as his right.

"It doesn't matter," Poklé thought, desperately trying to cheer himself up. He stopped in at a café on Place Paul-Signac for a glass of red wine. "After all, the *Mona Lisa* is all that matters. If this thing comes off and that crazy Greek snaps at the bait, I'll be my own man, my own boss. All my worries will vanish without a trace. And I'll take the boys to the coast, to Nice. The boys? Oh, God, I forgot about them again! They'll be dead by now!"

"If I may say, Mr. Poklé," remarked the café owner when the painter was paying for his wine, "you have a strange haircut. I barely recognize you."

The painter ground his teeth and hurried toward Rue Bretonneau. How could he have forgotten that it was Friday, and the thirteenth to boot? Why had the boys arrived today, of all days? And why had he let them go hungry today, of all days?

"I haven't even given them any hemp," the painter thought disconsolately.

He ran up the stairs, reached his apartment, and unlocked the door. He was astonished to find the apartment empty. Koko and Zlatko should have returned from the barber some time ago. They had made plans to take a walk together before dinner.

"I hope nothing went wrong. Today is Friday, the thirteenth, their first day in Paris, and I let them wander about the city on their own. No wonder they left! I must have spent three hours at that butcher's. I must be out of my mind. What would my sister say if anything happened to them? I must be mad, mad. I'm really overdoing it with the *Mona Lisa*. I can think of nothing but the *Mona Lisa* and the Greek."

As soon as he remembered the painting, Poklé was transformed. He tugged at the feeble remnants of his beard and forgot again about the boys and their hunger. He cast a blissful glance up toward the attic.

"Good heavens," he yelled. He wanted to grab his beard but instead clutched his throat. "What is this?"

The four padlocks on the doors leading to his attic studio were unlocked; the keys were hanging down loosely.

"Naughty boys," the painter said with mounting trepidation. "How did they ever find the keys? Inspector Maigret himself couldn't have found them. I wonder what they were doing up there? Of course, they may still be up there. They may have gone up there and fainted from hunger. Let's see."

But Zlatko and Koko were not in the attic. They were not on the balcony either. Poklé was about to go back downstairs when his eyes rested on the black curtain.

"I'll just take a quick look. I can't resist looking at her. Not many people have the *Mona Lisa* in their apartments."

He turned the light on and walked over. He lifted up all three curtains, the black, the red, and the white. And then he fainted flat on the floor.

When he finally came to, a half hour had passed. With shaky legs he walked over to the curtain. He didn't bother to lift it. He didn't have the courage. He just stroked it. No, he hadn't made a mistake. His fingers didn't feel anything hard. There was no doubt about it: the painting was not there.

"Police! Police!" the painter yelled and started to rush down the stairs. "Police!"

But then he grabbed his throat again and grew uncomfortably silent.

"I must be out of my mind. The police! That's all I need. What a story it would make! And what would the Greek say to that? And Alles Worson? I must calm down, collect my wits. But how can I? I'm finished. Destroyed. Friday the thirteenth, a black day! If someone were to write a book about me, this would be Chapter 13, the unhappy chapter. I'm done for! A mere nobody. I can't let this happen. I'll jump off the Eiffel Tower, of course. Right now is the best time."

But on second thought, perhaps all was not lost. True, he had been careless. He had inadvertently given the thieves an opportunity, but that didn't mean that the painting would not be found again. What would they do with it anyway? Besides, he thought maybe they won't start shooting the movie tomorrow. Maybe it's been postponed. And in the meantime, he would find the *Mona Lisa*.

He was barely able to dial Worson's number at his apartment on Avenue de la Bourdonnais.

"Right, Mr. Poklé. Of course we'll be shooting to-morrow. At eight o'clock, at the Louvre. I was about to call you to let you know that Mr. Worson would appreciate your bringing the painting a little before eight—at seven forty-five. Would that be possible?" the director's secretary asked graciously.

Poklé trembled from head to foot and put down the receiver with great care, as if it were a bomb about to go off. Then he began looking for Somais's telephone number. He dialed seven digits, but when he heard the sharp voice of Maurice, the old butler, he could not bring himself to talk. He hung up as fast as he could.

"It's best I don't call the Greek. He'll go out of his mind. He'll slice off my head with his cane. I may be able to get it all straightened out—who knows? If some-one has really stolen the *Mona Lisa,* he won't get very far . . . if . . ."

He climbed up into the attic again, to see if a miracle had happened and the *Mona Lisa* was back in its place. He had merely been tired, worried about the boys, un-happy over his ravaged beard, and as a result had im-agined that the painting wasn't there.

In three bounds he was back in the attic. He turned on all the lights in the studio and then gingerly walked over to the curtain. He lifted it. No miracle. The empty wall stared at him. There was no trace of the *Mona Lisa.*

Then suddenly he noticed that below, near the space where the *Mona Lisa* had hung, there was a white paper nailed to the wall. The painter picked it up and began to read.

Dear Uncle:
When you've read this, you can stop worrying. Nothing has happened. Koko got involved with armed gangsters who intend to kill him. Nothing dangerous, as I said, a mere trifle. That's Paris for you! They have threatened to bury him alive or throw him into the river unless they receive a large ransom. We made an agreement: I would give them your painting. Don't worry, I'll doublecross them. I know Paris. The poor idiots think this painting is the real thing. As soon as I have any news, I'll call you. Don't worry. Everything's fine. I'll take good care of the painting. Please don't jump off the Eiffel Tower until we come back with the painting. Best regards,

Yours,
Zlatko

The poor painter missed his beard more than ever and clutched his throat. Before fainting once again he said through his teeth, "Boys, what have you done to me? Oh, boys . . . the painting wasn't mine. Oh, if only I'd warned them, told them my own painting is at the Louvre and the one the kidnappers have is the original —the real Leonardo, the most famous and the most valuable painting in the world! I am done for. I must jump from the Eiffel Tower."

And for the second time that day the painter fainted.

Where's the police station?

14 When Koko rushed down the stairs in pursuit of the red car and the cripple, Zlatko had brushed the incident off contemptuously. But as time passed, he grew increasingly concerned.

Two hours later there was still no sign of either Koko or Uncle Poklé. Had Koko run into Poklé and were the two of them now walking around Paris?

Suddenly he heard a whining sound, at first low and distant and then louder, like a dog whose tail is being pulled. Zlatko laughed. It was his stomach! He must be very hungry.

"I'll bet Koko is starved too! He was so scared on the plane that he hardly ate a thing. Perhaps it was the hunger that made him hallucinate and imagine the painting had disappeared."

Zlatko felt a bit dizzy himself, so he decided to look around the apartment for something to eat. He remembered from the year before that his uncle kept food in

the closet under the attic stairs. But just as he was bend-
ing down to see what was in those little greasy bundles
and containers, the telephone rang. His first thought
was that something had happened to Koko.

"Hello," Zlatko shouted into the receiver.

"It's me. Koko. Me," stammered a voice at the other
end of the wire.

"Where are you? What are you doing? Stop playing
with me!" Zlatko screamed.

"I'm not, Zlatko. Honest. I've been kidnapped. It's
the first time for them, and for me, I mean . . ."

"What are you talking about? Calm down and tell me
where you are and what it's all about."

"I'm in the woods. Near a zoo. In the hands of kidnappers. They'll toss me into the lake, and if I drown,
for example, they'll bury me. No, I mean after they
bury me, they'll . . ."

"Koko, you've got to get hold of yourself," Zlatko
shouted.

"Listen, you must bring the *Cleopatra*."

"What Cleopatra?"

"Your uncle's painting, the woman with a smile."

"You mean the *Mona Lisa,* don't you, Koko?"

And so with a great deal of difficulty Koko managed
to explain to his old friend that his life depended on
whether he, Zlatko, would bring the painting to the kidnappers at the Porte Dorée subway station near the Bois
de Vincennes. He casually reminded Zlatko that he and

Zlatko were blood brothers and that he hoped Zlatko would not abandon him in his misfortune.

As soon as he hung up, Zlatko got down the painting and proceeded to wrap it up in old newspapers. He found some string and bound the painting up and down and crosswise. He left a message for his uncle on the wall and, with the *Mona Lisa* under his arm, he ran off toward the Pelleport station.

On his way down in the elevator to the subway, he concentrated so hard that his jaws ached. Somehow or other, he was convinced, he would figure out a way of bringing both Koko and the painting back home.

By the time he got on the third and last train, the one that would finally take him to the Bois de Vincennes, he had cooked up a plan.

When he got off at Porte Dorée, he took a deep breath of fresh air and surveyed the territory. In the distance he saw the Nautical Museum; behind it stretched a dark forest, and deep inside the forest was the zoo.

Zlatko crossed the street and walked over to a man standing at the opposite corner, a strong young man with thick eyebrows and a little moustache.

"Excuse me, sir, I'm a stranger in Paris. Could you tell me where the nearest police station is?"

"Why? What happened?" the young man asked and arched his brows.

Zlatko briefly explained what had happened to Koko. The young man laughed.

"Oh, well, that's very funny. They're obviously inexperienced kidnappers. But you're right, you should tell the police. There's a police station right over there, behind the museum. Come on, I'll show you the way."

"Oh, thank you very much," Zlatko said cheerfully, still clutching the *Mona Lisa* under his arm.

They passed the Nautical Museum and then turned into a dark alley. Zlatko thought he saw a little Citroën in the distance.

"I'm afraid that car is theirs, sir. Where is that police station?"

"There," the young man said, pointing into the darkness. "You see that light?"

Zlatko stared in the direction of the stranger's finger, but he could see nothing. At that instant he felt the pressure of a sharp object on his back and a bony hand covering his mouth. Before he had a chance to yell, he was lying in the grass next to the pavement; the young man was kneeling on his chest and holding his hand on his mouth so tightly that Zlatko could barely breathe. He had dropped the *Mona Lisa,* and it was lying on the grass. There wasn't a soul around. A long sharp object glistened in the attacker's hand.

"I'm done for," Zlatko thought. "This is the end."

After the man had turned him over on his stomach, stuffed a handkerchief in his mouth, and tied his hands behind his back, he let Zlatko get up and pushed him ahead. He picked up the painting and followed Zlatko, prodding him in the back from time to time with that sharp, shiny object.

"You got him, didn't you, Jean?" Michel said cheerfully from where he stood in front of the car in which poor frightened Koko was sitting.

"I was right, of course," said Jean. "I knew he was going to try and play a trick on us. 'Excuse me, sir. Where's the police station?' And me—bang! There's your police station! Get into the car!"

And so Koko and Zlatko were together again, this time inside the old Citroën. Michel sat in the back with Koko, and Zlatko, the handkerchief removed but his hands tied, was in the front with Jean.

"You got us into a nice stew," Zlatko said, turning to look at Koko and speaking in Serbo-Croatian. "What made you get involved with these gangsters?"

"I mean . . . all that counts now is to stay alive. I mean," Koko stammered, softly scratching behind the ear.

"What do you think my uncle will say when he finds out that the painting's gone? It would be easier for us to go back without our heads than without the *Mona Lisa*. Why did you have to tell them we had the painting? Why, Koko, why?"

"They think it's the real thing. They don't know your uncle painted it."

"Shut up," Zlatko hissed. "If they find that out, we're done for."

But Jean didn't like to hear them speaking a language he didn't understand. "You two are to speak French when you're with us. Is that clear?"

"This Mongol's very funny looking," said Michel, grabbing the remaining tuft of hair on Zlatko's head. "You've got a great haircut, old man, like Genghis Khan. Is that the new style in your country?"

"That's enough, Michel," said Jean, lighting a cigarette. "Business is business. We've got to act fast."

Michel tore off a piece of newspaper wrapping from the painting.

"Hey, look at this! This is the real thing! Even if I knew math as well as my teacher, I'd never be able to figure out how much it's worth. We've got it, haven't we, Jean? If that crazy shipowner was willing to pay a shipful of money for *Cleopatra,* surely he'll cough up a billion for the *Mona Lisa.* He'll keep it hidden in his attic and look at it every night, and, of course, he won't be able to show it to anyone. If someone accidentally finds out what's cooking, the Greek'll tie him up in the attic and let him starve to death, right, Jean? They're making a film at the Louvre that's based on our story. Did you know that?"

"You remember what the cripple said? It'll be hard for us to get the money. But who cares about the money?"

"The cripple doesn't know a thing. If he had the *Mona Lisa* in his hands, I wonder how he'd feel?"

The cripple! Zlatko and Koko were dumbfounded,

and Zlatko realized that perhaps Koko was not nearly as crazy as he had first seemed. Perhaps Koko's story about the painting's temporarily disappearing from the wall was true after all. He suddenly remembered his earlier theory that hunger had deranged Koko's mind. He turned to Jean and roared, "We're hungry! Terribly hungry! We haven't eaten all day. If we get sick, you'll be responsible. That's all there's to it."

"The Mongolians are hungry," Michel said cheerfully, giggling. "Did you get that, Jean? We'll have to feed them!"

"Yes, Michel," Jean said, "he's right. We've got to look after them. You'll just have to be patient, boys. As soon as we've taken care of the business part of this job, we'll feed you."

"Listen, Jean," Koko said. "You said you'd let me go as soon as you got the painting. What are you waiting for?"

"We've been had," Zlatko said bitterly.

"Don't be naive, Mongol," said Michel, narrowing his eyes. "What do you expect us to do? You want us to let you go so that you can run to the first cop with your sob story. Very clever. You tried it once before, didn't you? So who's cheating, you or us?"

"Ah, well," grunted Zlatko.

"Don't argue, boys," Jean said in a conciliatory tone. "Michel, you shouldn't poke fun at them, and Koko and Zlatko will understand that they have to help us. If they'd kidnapped us in their country, I'd help them. We have problems too, Koko. We don't kidnap foreigners every day, and we don't steal paintings every day."

"Ah, well," said Zlatko.

"Anyway," Jean continued, "I've got a plan. Michel, you're going to call up the Greek right now."

"Me?" Michel was stunned. "Why me? My voice isn't deep enough. The shipowner won't take me seriously. He'll see through us right away."

"You'll have to make your voice sound important, that's all. This was your idea in the first place. Stuff a piece of Kleenex in your mouth, or something. Meanwhile, I'll watch our two friends. That clear? As soon as you've completed the negotiations, you'll buy a couple of thick sandwiches for them at the nearest café and two bottles of Coke. Understand?"

"O.K.," Michel agreed reluctantly. "What do I say to the Greek, though?"

Zlatko and Koko exchanged glances while Jean and Michel negotiated the amount they should ask from the rich shipowner. They finally agreed that asking a piddling ten million francs for such a famous painting would be almost giving it away, but that they would settle for it. Michel walked over to a nearby telephone booth.

The three boys sat in the dark. Jean smoked, and Koko thought how extraordinary it was that at this time last night he was getting ready for bed in his own room, saying good-bye to the beautiful locust tree under his window. His heart suddenly felt very heavy, and he said the first thing that came to mind, "Listen, Zlatko, we're so close to the zoo now. Couldn't we take a look at those sharks, please?"

"You're mad," Zlatko said crossly. He had other ideas on his mind. The more he thought about his uncle, the more mystified he was about Poklé's handling of the famous painting from which he expected so much and on which he said his whole life depended.

The most serious conversation in the world

15   In a dark corner of the shipowner's large garden, Katsarida bent down swiftly and picked up a little packet from the pebble-covered path. He cautiously looked around, afraid that someone might be watching him, and quickly stuffed it into his pocket.

He walked over to a still more secluded spot, took the packet out, and turned on his flashlight. It was a piece of paper weighted down by a small rock. He unfolded the paper and found a message written in large bold letters:

A. POKLÉ
PAINTER
3 RUE BRETONNEAU
TEL: PEL 24-38

"That Marie, she's a little devil," Katsarida thought in admiration. "She's right. She's a born spy. How did she manage to get the address?"

The boy threw the rock away and stuffed the precious message deep into his pocket.

It was with a heavy heart that Katsarida admitted to himself that it was this girl who had hatched this whole scheme. Marie's plan had been to find first the address of the man who had painted the new *Mona Lisa*, then his phone number, so that Katsarida could call him up, faking his father's voice, and ask a few questions (Katsarida would have to decide ahead of time what questions to ask). If the painter was not surprised by this call, if it turned out that he knew the shipowner well and that he was expecting to hear from him, it would mean that their suspicions were entirely justified. There would be no doubt left at all that once again the shipowner was involved in a risky adventure, this time with the most famous and the most expensive painting in the world.

"Easy enough for her," Katsarida thought, full of concern, as he walked into his room. "After all, it's not her father. I wouldn't be all that pleased to find that my father is involved in such a dirty business."

"Crack," the parrot said in greeting.

Katsarida stared at the colorful parrot for a minute, and the parrot stared right back at him. Ever since he had been brought back from the great bird exhibition, at which he won a second prize and a silver medal, the parrot's behavior had been very odd. He'd never stared at people like that before, and he certainly had never talked so much. Katsarida stroked him, and the bird fluttered his wings in an unfriendly response.

"Ah, well," Katsarida thought, "I can't worry about the parrot now. I've got more important things on my mind. People change, so why shouldn't parrots?"

The boy tiptoed to the telephone. His hands shook as he took out of his pocket the slip of paper with the telephone number.

"Mr. Poklé, Mr. Poklé." He mumbled the name to himself as if trying to memorize it. "Mr. Poklé, PEL 24-38." Then, aloud, he said, "Hello, is that you, Mr. Poklé? This is Somais speaking, yes . . ."

"Louder!" commanded the parrot.

"This is Somais," Katsarida said, this time much louder, and then he realized that he had obeyed the parrot's orders, and he shook his head. "My father's voice's much deeper. Perhaps I ought to speak through my fist, like this . . ."

And just as the boy put his fist to his mouth, the telephone rang. Who could it be? The parrot glared at the telephone with a look of great curiosity. Katsarida lifted the receiver and, in great confusion, said, "Hello . . . Poklé . . ."

"Yes, that's me. How . . . how . . . how did you guess?" stammered the painter at the other end. "How did you guess it was me, Mr. Somais?"

"Well, I thought around this time . . ." the boy blabbered, his knees shaking as if he had just turned the finest Alpine hairpin curve on his bike. Needless to say, he forgot all about speaking in a deep voice. On the contrary, his voice sounded squeakier than the parrot's.

The most serious conversation in the world [131]

"Something terrible has happened, Mr. Somais. I'm a lost man. I'll have to kill myself," the painter whispered dismally at the other end.

"Don't do that, Mr. Poklé. That's hardly necessary," Katsarida squeaked, not really knowing what to say.

"You have no idea," the poor painter went on. "I'm a lost man. The painting's disappeared."

"The *Mona Lisa?*" Katsarida said.

"Yes, the *Mona Lisa*. But you don't understand. It isn't my painting that's disappeared, but the real one, Leonardo's, the original! I'm done for. It was stolen. Not stolen, no, but used in a kidnapping! Don't ask me what the original was doing in my flat, Mr. Somais. Don't ask, please! Please! I'll explain everything later. I know I shouldn't have called you at this hour, I know you are a suspect . . ."

"Shhhh," the boy said, by now somewhat in control of himself. "Be careful what you say, Poklé!"

"I know, I know, Mr. Somais. But what can I do? I didn't really want to call you, but I didn't know what else to do, honestly. I can't very well turn to the police."

"Shhhh," Katsarida hissed. "Of course not. Wait for me to call you, Poklé. I'll think of something. I'll let you know what to do next. And don't call me here. I have told you this before. I'll call you."

"Of course. I understand, Mr. Somais. Thank you. Thank you very much. I'll wait. I'll wait. You'll forgive me, won't you? I didn't know. Good night, Mr. Somais. Forgive me, won't you?"

"Good night, Poklé, and don't worry," said the boy, by now altogether calm. He put down the receiver.

"Crack," said the parrot.

The boy worked his fingers through his thick hair and looked out of the window and into the night.

"Why did I have to get involved?" he thought frantically. "What have I gotten involved in? Why do I get mixed up in things that are no good for me? My father insists that I read Homer's *Iliad* and that I play the piano, and I just want to read magazines and ride a bike. If he wants me to play an instrument, it'll have to be an electric guitar, I said. But he won't hear of it. And now Marie Cléver wants me to become a detective."

Then, aloud, he said to the parrot, "That's not for me, right, César?"

"Good night, Poklé," screeched the parrot.

"You'll give me away, you scavenger," Katsarida shouted, and he drew back his arm to strike the bird, but stopped himself. "You feathered idiot," he mumbled, and retreated into a corner of his room and sat down on a pile of magazines, determined to think this out.

No sooner had he sat down than he had to jump up. The telephone was ringing again. The parrot screeched, "Crack." The boy couldn't understand who would be calling again this late at night, or why Maurice, the butler, wasn't answering the phone downstairs, as was the custom in the shipowner's household. But the phone continued to ring, and Katsarida finally lifted the receiver himself.

"May I please speak to Mr. Somais, the shipowner?" a deep male voice inquired from the other end.

The boy quickly put his hand to his mouth and bellowed into the receiver, "Somais speaking. Who's this?"

"Who cares? I'm calling in the name of a band of kidnappers. We know what you're after, Mr. Somais, and we'd like to make you a business proposition. All we have to do is agree on the price. The *Mona Lisa* is in our possession, and we're offering it to you," said the voice frantically as it sank lower and lower. By now it sounded as though it were coming from the bottom of a barrel.

"The *Mona Lisa!*" Katsarida thundered into the receiver. "Where did you find her?"

"I mean the painting not the woman," the deep voice echoed.

This was the most serious conversation that had passed through the telephone wires since Alexander Bell invented the instrument.

"Louder!" shouted the parrot.

"What do you want from me now?" roared Katsarida.

"Let's not play games, Mr. Somais," the other voice bellowed. "We know you well. We know all about the *Cleopatra* affair. We know that such a valuable painting can't be sold on the free market because no one would dare buy it. But there are people like you, Mr. Somais, who love famous paintings so much that they don't mind coughing up millions so they can have them hanging in some cellar where they can admire them all by themselves . . ."

"O.K. But what do you want from me now?"

"Only ten million francs, Mr. Somais, and the *Mona Lisa* is yours."

"Only how much?" Katsarida choked slightly.

"Ten million francs is a pittance for a painting that's worth a billion dollars. You know that, Mr. Somais, and you know that a film is being made on this very subject."

"Have it your way," Katsarida finally said in despair because he actually didn't know what else to say. "Have it your way, I say. Bring the painting here."

"To your house, you mean? Out of the question. You don't think we're that naive, do you? A trap, ha? Get the money ready by tomorrow morning and we'll make arrangements where to meet. Not indoors. In the street. The earlier in the morning the better, before there are too many people around."

"How's eight o'clock?"

"Too late. Make it seven. And you decide on the place. Somewhere in your neighborhood."

"There's a barbershop at Place d'Auteuil. Let's meet there. In front of it. I think it's called FRÉDÉRIC's. Will you remember that?"

"Of course, Mr. Somais. My best friend's old man is called Frédéric."

"How will we recognize one another?"

"That's easy, Mr. Somais. All you have to do is to bring the dough at seven o'clock. In front of FRÉDÉRIC's. We know you. We've seen your picture in the papers

The most serious conversation in the world [135]

a number of times with your cane."

"Good," Katsarida concluded in a hoarse voice. "Fine."

"But no tricks, Mr. Somais," Michel said breathlessly. He couldn't wait to hang up, remove the handkerchief from his mouth, and breathe fresh air again. "Our people will be watching you from the neighboring roof."

"Fine, fine," said Katsarida hopelessly. "See you tomorrow."

"See you tomorrow, Mr. Somais," Michel babbled and finally hung up.

Katsarida continued to stare at the telephone.

"Fine, fine. Nothing's fine. Nothing at all. What am I going to do? What?"

The invisible sign

I 6 The night Koko and Zlatko spent in the car was not particularly pleasant, but it could have been worse. They almost became friends with the kidnappers. After the telephone conversation with the Greek, Michel brought them four enormous ham sandwiches, which they washed down with two bottles of Coke. After this ample supper, the darkness in the Bois de Vincennes no longer seemed so ominous.

When the time came for them to go to sleep, Koko and Zlatko stayed inside the car. They weren't exactly sorry not to be outside, in the dark forest. Jean and Michel took turns watching them. While one of them kept an eye on the car, the other stretched out on a nearby park bench.

"What do you say, Zlatko? How do you think we'll get out of here?"

"You're a terrific bore, Koko. How can you be such a coward? You only think about yourself. I'm thinking about something else."

"What's bothering you, Zlatko?"

"Ah, well, I feel sorry for my uncle. He's a strange man. Like most artists, I guess. But there's something else there too. You remember him saying, 'It's a deadly secret. My whole future is tied up in it. If I make a lot of money, as I suspect I will, I can paint anything I want.' He threatened to jump from the Eiffel Tower if this deal fell through. Get it, Koko?"

"Get it," said Koko, feeling so tired that his eyelids felt like lead.

"You don't understand anything," said Zlatko. He was discouraged. "I'm afraid my uncle's involved in some dangerous game. Perhaps he promised to get the original *Mona Lisa* for someone. This may all be a fraud. The movie may only be an excuse to exchange the paintings, don't you see? That's why he's hoping for so much money. If he doesn't succeed, if they catch him, then he'll have to jump off the Eiffel Tower."

"Mm," Koko mumbled. He was already three-quarters asleep.

"Michel and Jean may have gotten mixed up in this whole mess by accident. Maybe. Maybe not. Who knows? They did mention the cripple. The cripple! He's the most mysterious person in all this. Jean and Michel may be working for him. Of course, there may be some other gang working against them. My poor uncle."

Koko was asleep.

"There's no one I can talk to or ask for advice," and

Zlatko turned over in his seat, closed his eyes tight, hoping to fall asleep as soon as possible.

The sun rose high above the Bois de Vincennes. It was a beautiful bright morning.

Jean knocked on the car window, and both boys were instantly aroused from their deep sleep. Koko was sure he was still dreaming, and Zlatko stretched his long legs and tightened his jaw in anticipation of a hard day.

"On your feet, parasites," Michel greeted them cheerfully. "It's past six o'clock, and by seven we have to be at the other end of Paris."

"You'll be free in a little while," said Jean.

"It's about time," said Zlatko as unpleasantly as he could.

"Mongol's fuming," said Michel and narrowed his eyes.

"That's enough," Jean cut in. "Get into the car. Let's go to Place d'Auteuil."

"I'm hungry," said Koko. "At home my mother gives me milk, bread, and butter the minute I'm up."

"Look here, Koko," Michel exploded. "Are you suggesting I should run all over Paris at six o'clock in the morning looking for your breakfast? You're out of your mind, old man. You two guys happen to be kidnapped, and you're behaving as if you were on a field trip and we're your teachers."

"Shut up, Michel. Get into the car," Jean yelled.

And all five of them, the four boys and the *Mona Lisa,* got into the little Citroën. Jean turned the motor on, coasted gently from the grass onto the street, and drove off to meet new adventures.

Michel noticed with what great curiosity Koko looked out at the city streets, and he commented sadly, "You're lucky, you guys. Paris is marvelous for you. But it's old hat to me. We've seen every one of these streets a hundred times. I'm as fed up with Paris as you guys must be with Zagreb."

Koko did like Paris, but he couldn't quite go along with the theory that his own city was boring. Yet he thought it wiser not to say anything. The Seine seemed so narrow when they crossed it. Hadn't Zlatko said it was so wide that you couldn't see from one side to the other? Or did he dream that? Perhaps here they were close to its source, and further downstream it was as wide as five Savas and three Danubes.

"I have a feeling, boys"—Zlatko was suddenly grave —"that something's bothering you. Perhaps you were really looking forward to going away this summer. Now you have to stay in Paris, and you are so angry that you don't know what to do with yourselves."

"Fantastic," said Jean, and he turned to Michel enthusiastically. "This Mongol is damn clever."

Jean lit a cigarette and then slowly described his own and Michel's problem. He said how much he'd hoped to see the glorious castles along the Loire and how much his friend had hoped to see the coast, and how their fathers, Frédéric and Charles, had backed out on their promises at the last minute. And to think how hard Jean and Michel had worked in school to get good grades!

The little car was speeding through the streets of Paris, which were still relatively deserted. They drove under an overpass and saw a train rushing past. Michel explained that where the underground trains emerged like that it's called the "air railway." Then Jean pointed out the Citroën factory, where cars like the one they were in were manufactured. Then they crossed the Seine once again and entered the southwest part of Paris. It was twelve minutes to seven.

The car was already speeding along Rue d'Auteuil in the direction of their rendezvous with the wealthy ship-owner. Jean and Michel no longer paid any attention to their prisoners. At Place Jean-Lorrain Jean slammed his foot on the brake and mumbled, "How odd! I thought that beyond this square Rue d'Auteuil was one way and that I had to take a side street off to the right to get to Place d'Auteuil."

"Maybe they changed it. There's no sign," said Michel, squirming uncomfortably in his seat. "Go right ahead. I can't wait. The old tightwad may have called the police. Who knows?"

"No. Out of the question," said Jean. "He can only think of the *Mona Lisa.*"

But before he even completed his sentence, he brought the car to such a sudden stop that the boys bounced forward like balls. Some hundred feet ahead there were four policemen; they stood there as if waiting for the boys.

"Get out and take the painting with you," Jean whispered as if afraid the policemen might overhear him. "Fast. If I get out of this, I'll be right back to get you."

Zlatko, Koko, and Michel tumbled out of the car. Zlatko had the precious possession under his arm. Jean stepped on the accelerator and drove off.

At Place Jean-Lorrain the milk bars were open, and forgetting for a while the seriousness of the moment, Koko licked his lips at the thought of a nice big glass of milk.

"Koko's terribly hungry, Michel," Zlatko said severely. "He's anemic, and he faints if he doesn't get a pint of milk and two buns first thing in the morning. You're responsible for him, you know. He'll give you trouble. That's not what you need right now, is it?"

"For God's sake," Michel said, fuming, but then he saw an open door to a milk bar and shrugged his shoulders. "O.K., I suppose I'll have to get him his milk if he can't live without it. That's what we get for dealing with babies."

Koko was about to object, but Zlatko stepped on his toe. Michel strode angrily into a milk bar, unable to understand how anyone could think of milk at a time like this and, in his fury, forgetting that he had left his two captives alone with the precious painting. At that very moment Bus No. 52 stopped before a red light. Zlatko

grabbed Koko by the sleeve and pushed him onto the bus. When Michel came out of the milk bar with a glass of milk, he saw, to his absolute astonishment, the bus and the two captives disappearing in the direction from which they had come a few minutes earlier. He dropped the glass on the pavement and swore through his teeth.

Meanwhile, the four policemen on Rue d'Auteuil, not far from Place d'Auteuil and Frédéric's barbershop, stopped Jean's car.

"Good morning," said the first policeman sternly.

"You realize you're driving the wrong way," said the second policeman even more sternly.

"Your driver's license, please," said the third policeman angrily.

The fourth policeman said nothing.

"I myself was surprised to find there was no sign at the entrance to this street," Jean said calmly, enormously relieved that he had been stopped only because of a traffic violation.

The four policemen said nothing. They examined his license, looked over the car and its young driver. Then the fourth policeman said severely, "You will not object to our taking away your driver's license if we find the sign is there?"

"No, of course not," said Jean cheerfully.

The fourth policeman took Jean by the arm, and in a leisurely stride they walked in the direction of Place Jean-Lorrain, where Michel was paying at the milk bar for the broken glass.

"Well, now, what do you call this?" the policeman asked as they paused before the do-not-enter sign.

Jean arched his thick brows and shrugged. He could have sworn that the sign had not been there a few min-utes before. Moreover, he was convinced that someone was playing a trick on him. It was past seven o'clock, and by the time the police would finally let him go, Somais, the rich shipowner, would have long abandoned their rendezvous.

Millions of dollars in the air

17 "What now?" Koko asked.

"Don't worry. Just get off the bus. We're on a busy street. We won't get lost," Zlatko replied.

The bus had taken them along a route that was very different from the one that Jean had followed. He didn't like being in an unfamiliar area again. Getting lost once was enough.

"The best thing is to stay on the main streets; then you won't get lost," Zlatko said, as if reading his friend's thoughts. "I'm sure we're not very far from some central spot. See, I was right! I know exactly where we are."

"Why did we get off the bus in the first place?"

"Why? You really are dumb, Koko. Obviously, to throw them off our track. Don't you see? We'll get on the underground here, and that's that."

"What do you mean 'that's that'? Where are we going?"

"Listen, Koko, are you asking these questions seriously,

or are you kidding? Obviously we are going right back to Pelleport so we can return the painting to my uncle."

Koko scratched behind his ear, and not for the first time came to the conclusion that it was best not to ask Zlatko too many questions.

They had reached the Place du Trocadéro. On the south side of the square rose a white building divided in two wings. Zlatko was looking for the Métro sign that marks the entrance to the underground. Koko looked about uncomfortably. He had the feeling that someone's eyes were glued to his back, but he didn't dare say anything to Zlatko.

They crossed the street and found themselves between the two wings of the white building: Koko's heart stopped beating for a moment. There, in the distance, across several terraces, parks, fountains, and pools of water framed by the two wings of the white building, on the other side of the Seine rose the gigantic Eiffel Tower like an iron giraffe.

"Let's go up there! To the top of the Eiffel Tower!" Koko said enthusiastically.

"Koko," Zlatko reprimanded him. "Don't be ridiculous. First we've got to take the painting back to my uncle. My uncle'll . . ."

"Your uncle'll jump off the Eiffel Tower, Zlatko!" Koko retorted cheerfully. "Didn't he say that was what he would do if things went wrong with the *Mona Lisa*. He may be up there right now, you know."

"Now?" Zlatko asked, absorbed in thought. Perhaps Koko's suggestion was not as ridiculous as it sounded.

"Come on, Zlatko," Koko insisted. "Who knows if we'll have another chance, the way things have been going. We may be kidnapped again. Listen, Zlatko," he recalled suddenly, "you said one could see all of Paris from up there . . ."

"Nonsense!" Zlatko cut him off.

"And you said," Koko went on undaunted, "that through binoculars you could see into every nook and cranny. Every house, for example. Didn't you say that?"

"Maybe I did," Zlatko said uncertainly. "Of course I did. So what?"

"In that case, why can't we find your uncle with a pair of binoculars?" Koko jumped up in excitement. "Don't you see? At least we can find out if he's home."

"O.K. O.K. Let's go," said Zlatko, shaking his head. "You sure have funny ideas. You think Paris is a village. Like your Green Hill. O.K., you'll see it now! But I'll tell you one thing: you have no idea what Paris is like."

Koko was bubbling with excitement as they approached the colossal iron tower. But Zlatko's mind was preoccupied with other things. Perhaps up there, in the fresh air, he might be able to think more clearly and solve the riddles that weighed on his mind so. In any case, it would do no harm to take time out before taking the next step.

When they finally stood under the four giant legs of

the Eiffel Tower, Koko's neck was already hurting from the strain of looking up. Zlatko counted out the change left over from yesterday's haircuts and decided that they didn't have enough to buy elevator tickets. They would have to climb. "He'll see," Zlatko thought maliciously. "That's what he gets for wanting to go up the tower. He'll find out what Paris is all about."

And what a climb it was! Koko would never forget it. At first it felt as if he were on the roof of his house, from where he happily flew paper planes, but soon it began to feel uncomfortable and dangerous—even worse than on the plane. The cars on the avenues below grew smaller and smaller; people looked like fleas. How many hundreds of steps did they have to climb to get to the first landing? And the next one after that?

"Don't look down," Zlatko said. "It'll make you dizzy. Either look straight ahead or up."

"O.K.," Koko said. He was almost green by now. To make matters worse, it was his own idea, and he couldn't very well protest now.

"You know something?" Zlatko suddenly said, clutching the painting under his arm. "We've got to think through this whole mess with the *Mona Lisa* very carefully. Especially the part my uncle plays in it all, and the shipowner, and that cripple—he's really important, I'm sure of it. And we've got to figure out where we stand and what we should do now."

Koko sighed. By now he had developed a whole set of new worries. He suddenly imagined that his leg would get stuck in the space between the two iron threads and that he wouldn't be able to get loose and that he would hang suspended like a bat above that horrible abyss.

"Now if my uncle's *Mona Lisa* was picked from among so many entries," Zlatko thought aloud, "as the one that was closest to the original, then it's obvious that the picture and the man who painted it got a lot of publicity. So, obviously, that's where the whole thing begins. And where does that lead us? To that rich crazy Greek shipowner Somais, who is prepared to pay a gigantic sum of money to get hold of the *Mona Lisa*."

"Oh, my God!" Koko yelped as he tripped on a step.

"Don't be a bore, Koko! Anyway, my uncle probably knew that. That leaves us with two things we have to figure out now, Koko. First: maybe my uncle got involved with the Greek and decided to help him get the original *Mona Lisa* by exchanging it for his good copy. Or maybe some gang headed by the cripple is trying to fool my uncle, who knows nothing about the shipowner, in order to get the *Mona Lisa* and sell it for a vast sum of money. Also, they may be trying to put all the blame on my uncle. But my uncle talked about it so much and had such high hopes that I'm afraid he may be mixed up. Which leaves us with this question: Should we help him, Koko, or shouldn't we? Imagine that the exchange has already taken place and that what we're lugging up here with us is the original. Wow!"

"Fine," said poor Koko, as perspiration dripped down his nose. "I'd like to go back down."

The next minute Koko wished he had never said what he had because Zlatko delivered him a lecture such as he had never heard before in his life. Zlatko might even have hit him had there been more room and if a number of other people had not been following them up the stairs. He reminded Koko that this whole climb had been his own idea, that he hadn't wanted to come, and he threatened never to talk to him again if he didn't sober up now. Koko was so upset that his nose began to bleed.

By the time they'd reached the first landing, both boys had calmed down considerably. The climb to the next landing went much faster and without a word. Koko was green in the face, Zlatko was red.

"Here you are. Now, look!" Zlatko said when they finally reached the second landing. "That's Paris!"

What a fabulous sight! What a fantastic maze of streets, squares, monuments, bridges, parks, tree-lined avenues—all stretching as far as the eye could see. And the traffic echoed louder than the worst summer thunderstorm. For a moment Koko forgot his fright and nausea and Zlatko his anger and worries. Zlatko pointed out the most famous spots, and the area in which his uncle lived. Off to the west, beyond the Bois de Boulogne, it was raining; here the sun was shining.

"Let's look through the binoculars," Koko proposed enthusiastically.

"You can't see that far. You're such a dummy, Koko," Zlatko objected. "Paris is enormous. Pelleport is a good ten miles from here."

"But we may still be able to see him somewhere—your uncle, I mean. He may be on his way here," Koko insisted.

"O.K., go ahead. Look while the money lasts!" Zlatko barked and dropped a coin into the binoculars.

Koko quickly gripped the huge instrument, which turned with difficulty on its base, and looked out at Paris. Although some structures, such as the Arc de Triomphe and the Louvre, appeared much closer, he quickly understood that he would never be able to find Poklé there. There were so many people at the foot of the tower that he wouldn't be able to single out Zlatko's uncle even if he were to look for ten days.

So Koko decided to look at the windows of the neighboring building, which the binoculars brought closer to his eye. He saw men at their desks, women at their typewriters. Through one window he saw a dentist with a pair of pliers, and a shiver went down his spine.

And then Koko yelled so loudly that some hundred people turned to look at the two boys. Zlatko tapped him on the head.

"You're out of your mind, Koko!" Zlatko said furiously.

"Look! Look!" Koko stammered, passing the binoculars to Zlatko with a trembling hand.

"You're such a bore. What is it?" Zlatko said. And he grabbed the instrument that Koko tried to keep in the same position to make sure his friend could see what he had seen.

Zlatko leaned the painting against the guard rail, closed his left eye, and reluctantly put his right eye to the binoculars that Koko had directed toward a house located along a wide avenue to the east of the Eiffel Tower.

"Well," Zlatko said indifferently. "So?"

Then in front of the first-floor window of a large house on the Avenue de la Bourdonnais, Zlatko saw an unusual sight. A helicopter hung suspended like a huge butterfly pinned to the pages of a collector's album. A man with a black beard and a yellow cap on top of his dark head emerged from the helicopter and stretched out a leg toward the windowsill.

"What do you say? A madman?" said Koko triumphantly.

"What?" Zlatko responded, still apparently calm. But before he let go of the binoculars he memorized the address: 23 Avenue de la Bourdonnais. He thought that perhaps, at some point, this information might prove useful. "That's nothing, Koko. Just Paris. The streets are terribly busy, lots of traffic, cars moving slowly. And so people who are really busy take helicopters. Haven't I told you that before? Even telegrams are distributed by helicopters here, you know."

"I see," said Koko. He was disappointed. What can one say to a friend who doesn't get excited even by people stepping out of helicopters in the middle of nowhere? And he scratched behind his ear.

He scratched behind his ear so awkwardly that his elbow brushed the painting Zlatko had rested on the parapet. Like a large paper plane, the *Mona Lisa* began to descend into the abyss.

18 Poklé had joined the hundreds of curious spectators outside the Louvre on Saturday morning. People were eager to observe what they could of the preparations for the filming of *A Million-Dollar Painting*.

Spotlights, miles of cable, and heavy equipment were unloaded from cars and trucks. As time passed, the minor actors arrived and headed straight for dressing rooms, where they were met by barbers, hairdressers, and makeup people. At exactly 8 A.M. Alles Worson arrived. A tall man with a thick black beard that hid almost his entire face, Worson wore a pair of huge dark glasses and a little yellow cap. Just after nine a wave of applause signaled the arrival of the famous actor Tom O'Pool, and a few minutes later the beautiful Veronica Mitty put in an appearance.

Then Poklé and the other spectators outside became aware of a commotion, and Alles Worson burst out the door and drove off in a big car.

"He must have had a fight with his actors," one person said.

"It's not that," someone else volunteered. "I got the story from an electrician. Some painter was supposed to bring a copy of the *Mona Lisa* for the shooting, but the painter hasn't shown up and Worson's furious. He might do anything now."

A pale man with a strangely cropped beard, a large scar on his cheek, and a beret on his head was working his way through to the front of the crowd.

"What did you say?" he asked softly. "What did you say? Why did Worson stomp out of the museum?"

"He's looking for a painting," came the reply.

"No, not for the painting, but for the painter who had the audacity not to bring the painting."

"Why should Worson be looking for him?" someone else commented. "Nobody can make a fool of Alles Worson and get away with it. I saw a pistol in his pocket. He's going to kill the painter for being late."

"It would be just like him," added a voice from the crowd. "They say that when Worson shoots, he shoots to kill. Ha, ha, ha."

The man with the scar rolled his eyes, swayed, and fainted.

A young girl with brown hair and gray eyes stamped her foot and yelled, "Water! Bring some water! Why are you staring like sheep? Can't you see that man's sick?"

Several people ran off to get water. Others, astonished,

stared at the young girl who was ordering grownups around with such authority. And Marie Cléver triumphantly surveyed the curious crowd, happy that once again she was in the right place at the right time.

Just keep an eye on the painting

19 "I was simply not cut out to be a detective. I'm interested in bicycles, and I'd love to play the guitar," Katsarida thought sadly as he sipped Coca-Cola at the Café Malacoff, at the Place du Trocadéro, across the Seine from the Palais de Chaillot and the Eiffel Tower. "Marie Cléver got me into this mess. Of course, she loves it all."

After his telephone conversations with Poklé and the deep-voiced thief the night before, Katsarida had dashed off to see his friend Marie Cléver. He didn't have the courage to do anything on his own.

Marie Cléver was alone at home, that is if one didn't count the housekeeper and the large gray cat with orange eyes. Although Marie was busy at the typewriter when he arrived—she loved her father's typewriter— she greeted him very cheerfully. And, to make matters worse, she immediately knew what to do.

At her insistence, Katsarida phoned Poklé and introduced himself as a famous detective who already knew about the disappearance of the painting and who was ready to help him. The poor painter was deeply touched. The boy told him to be at Place d'Auteuil at seven o'clock sharp the following morning, where the thieves would attempt to sell the precious painting. A brown-haired girl by the name of Marie would meet him there, which would help to fool the gangsters. The invisible detective would be nearby and would make his appearance at the right moment.

But what had actually happened at seven o'clock sharp? Marie Cléver had met the painter, who hadn't had a wink of sleep all night. A few feet away, concealed in the doorway of a house on Rue d'Auteuil, was Katsarida. He had a camera with him. According to Marie's scheme, even if the painter didn't get the *Mona Lisa* back from the kidnappers, Katsarida would take a photo of the blackmailers from his hiding place—perhaps a photo of their car as well—which would be enough for the police to go on to track the kidnappers down within a few hours.

However, as so often happens in life, unforeseen circumstances had prevented the girl's clever plan from working. The thieves had driven the wrong way on a one-way street, and the police had stopped them. Katsarida had had no idea what to do when he saw two strange boys, Koko and Zlatko, disappearing into the distance with the painting. He hadn't dared to call out to Marie. She had told the painter that the famous detective was "somewhere nearby"—neglecting to mention that the distinguished professional would not be fifteen until the next day.

Of course we know what happened thereafter. Bus No. 52 had taken Koko and Zlatko from the scene, and Michel had dropped the glass of milk. The policemen, after an endless argument with Jean Brange, had finally piled into his car and driven him off. The painter had looked at his watch. Marie had looked very concerned, and Katsarida had finally decided to leave his hiding place to set out after the two boys who had vanished with the painting.

"Just keep an eye on the painting," Marie had warned him. "Whatever happens, don't lose sight of the painting. Also, try to photograph the person who has the painting. But, above all, watch the painting."

They had made arrangements to meet later at the Place du Trocadéro if they ran into difficulties. Under these circumstances Marie would bring the painter along, too, and introduce him to the young detective.

"To hell with it! I've simply got to go after them," Katsarida thought as Koko and Zlatko vanished from sight. He ran up Rue d'Auteuil, in the direction of Place Jean-Lorrain—in other words, in the same direction in which Koko and Zlatko had disappeared. He bumped into Michel, who was running in the opposite direction, looking for Jean to give him the horrible news that it was through his negligence that the two sly Yugoslavs had managed to escape with the painting.

And while Katsarida stood hopelessly in the small square, not knowing which way to turn, he felt someone gently tapping him on the shoulder.

"Young man," said a stranger with a wooden leg and a black patch over one eye, "if you're looking for the boys with a big package, I saw them on the No. 52 bus."

Forgetting to thank the stranger or to find out how he had guessed that he was indeed trying to catch up with the two boys with the stolen painting, Katsarida automatically jumped on the first No. 52 bus that came along. Then, of course, he realized that he had no idea where the thieves had gotten off, so he simply left the bus near Place du Trocadéro, where he had agreed to meet Marie.

As he reached Place du Trocadéro, he spotted two boys with a large bundle speeding off in the direction of the Eiffel Tower. Although he could barely tell the boys apart, he could clearly see the white object they carried: the large painting wrapped in newspaper. He took a photograph of them. He was almost sure that they would climb to the top of the tower, so he took a seat in the front row of tables at the Café Malacoff.

"I mustn't lose sight of the picture," Katsarida reminded himself, sipping the Coke he had ordered and keeping an eye on the white object slowly ascending the winding staircase of the Eiffel Tower.

In less than an hour Marie Cléver arrived. She was entirely out of breath.

"They're up there," Katsarida said to his friend triumphantly.

"Who?" Marie asked.

"The boys. The thieves, the thieves with the painting."

Katsarida explained to Marie that from this location he could constantly keep an eye on the painting and that as soon as they started coming down again, he would walk over to the Eiffel Tower and photograph them.

"The thieves may have decided to send the boys into the fire to save themselves," Marie said, trying hard to figure it out. "They may be sitting somewhere, watching it all, waiting to see what happens. What do you think?"

"I'm sure you're right, Marie," said Katsarida, looking with admiration straight into her large gray eyes. "You're always right, Marie."

The girl shrugged, slightly uncomfortable at being told that she was always right. Then she told Katsarida about her adventures with the painter, who insisted on going to the Louvre at all costs after they had failed to recover the painting from the thieves early that morning at Place d'Auteuil.

"I of course followed him to the Louvre and saw him faint when someone said Alles Worson would kill the painter who had failed to show up with the promised copy of the *Mona Lisa*. After Poklé got over his fainting spell, he wanted to go home—or rather to a café on Place Paul-Signac and have some wine. I went on the subway with him and realized we were being followed by an old couple—a somewhat stooped old man with a gray moustache and an old woman in a long black dress. Both had large old-fashioned spectacles on top of their noses. In fact, they looked like museum pieces. I had a hard time shaking them off, but I finally gave them the slip in the elevator at the Pelleport station."

"Marie, you're fantastic," said Katsarida.

"I left Poklé in his favorite café and told him to wait there for us," Marie went on. "But do you know what, Katsarida? That white dot up there is worth millions. That is the real *Mona Lisa*, you know. The painter told me that. He had already made the exchange, and the boys don't even realize what they've got. They think it's Poklé's creation. But you and I know better, don't we?"

"That's why my father . . ."

"Your father probably tried to get the original painting—with Mr. Poklé's assistance, of course. The painter put his copy in the Louvre, planning to sell the original to your father. But tell me, Katsar, what made you run off down Rue d'Auteuil like that?"

The boy told Marie the story of his adventures in minute detail, not forgetting to mention the cripple who sent him off on the right track.

"The cripple?" The girl was flabbergasted. "Who could he be working with, for heaven's sake? This whole mystery is hard to solve, even for my father." And she stamped her foot on the pavement. "But I'll manage. I'll show my father that I can manage better than he can. If he was fooled by the thieves into leaving town at the most critical time, I'm not going to be. I'll find out who those two old people were—old people, by the way, who run faster than our cat. Oh no, Marie Cléver never gives up. Mata Hari and Marie Cléver know no fear, know no mysteries they can't solve. I'm going to show my father that I'm not the little nitwit he takes me for."

"There's one more thing," said Katsarida, gazing complacently at the tips of his shoes and completely forgetting the *Mona Lisa* for a moment. "Something that could complicate matters still further."

"What?" said Marie hopefully, keeping an eye on the white dot in the distance instead of on the boy sitting across from her.

"When I came home last night from Rue Erlanger, you know, after I visited you, you know . . ."

"Stop stammering, Katsar. Think first and then speak. If it's important, that is."

"It's very important, Marie. I found it very strange, you know, that when I talked on the telephone to Poklé and the kidnappers that Maurice didn't pick up the call downstairs, but rather let the phone ring up in my room. It turns out that Maurice wasn't at home. Can you imagine, Marie?"

"So what?" said the girl. "What's so strange about that?"

"It's very strange, Marie. Maurice never goes out at night. He hasn't gone out in a long time—ten years at least. He's always home in the evening. But this time he wasn't."

"And?"

"And, you know, when I came home, I noticed the back entrance—you know the entrance we used to get into the garden shed— Well, I saw my father's new car parked there, and who should be using it but Maurice! He was very pale. Even in the dark I could tell that. He looked around like a hunted animal. Then he removed a long flat object, wrapped in paper, from the trunk. Just like a painting, you know. He turned around and said to someone in the car, 'Gently, gently, we must make sure that Katsarida doesn't see us. The light is still on in his room.' And he carried the object into the garden and I ran as fast as my legs would carry me and entered the house through the front door."

"Oh," Marie said condescendingly, swinging her legs from the bar stool, her eyes glued to the Eiffel Tower. "Are you trying to tell me that Maurice brought home still another *Mona Lisa*? Listen, there aren't *three* paintings around, just two. The original's at the top of the tower there, with the thieves; the false one is hanging in the Louvre, the one practically everyone thinks is the real one. But there just isn't any third. Nonsense, Katsar. That must have been something else. You were just imagining."

"But, Marie, Maurice wouldn't leave the house in the middle of the night for nothing and then sneak back in through the garden door!"

"Oh, my God!" the girl screamed and jumped up. "Look! Those madmen have dropped the *Mona Lisa* from the Eiffel Tower."

Katsarida turned his gaze in the direction of the iron tower, to which his friend's trembling hand was pointing.

And indeed, the most valuable painting in the world was slowly descending, like a large paper plane, from the top of the Eiffel Tower into the abyss below.

He shows his true colors

20 "Damnation!" roared the shipowner, banging his cane against the floor. The sharp pain in his leg caused him to frown. He walked over to the window and looked out anxiously. Thick clouds had gathered above the Bois de Boulogne. "Of course," he thought angrily, "it's going to rain. That's why my leg hurts."

His eyes rested again on the newspaper that he had tossed on the floor a moment before. He looked worried.

"Maurice!" the fat shipowner barked. "Maurice!"

Almost instantaneously the door opened wide and the old butler rushed in.

"The master wants me?"

"Maurice, you've betrayed me!" thundered Somais and banged his cane against the thick carpet.

"Master Somais!" the butler howled and hunched over even more. "How can you say such a thing?"

"You blabber too much. I'm sure you've told Katsarida everything."

"Absolutely not, sir. The young master was definitely in his room when we slipped in through the garden gate with the . . . so that . . ."

"That's not the point, Maurice, and you know it. I've known you for thirty-five years. I'm not asking you about last night. I want to know if you told Katsarida anything about that other matter—the *Mona Lisa,* I mean."

The old man bowed deeply, shook his head vehemently, and stammered, "No, never. I swear, sir."

"Then how come these damn journalists are poking into my affairs again? Why don't they leave me alone? Am I to blame that some idiots take it upon themselves to make a movie about the *Mona Lisa* at the same time as my biggest transatlantic ship is being completed?" the fat shipowner roared, banging his cane against the newspaper that lay limp on the carpet. It was a copy of *Le Clairon du Soir* with an article by Marcel Cléver headlined "The Theft of the *Mona Lisa* from the Louvre."

"It's not my fault, sir. I don't know anything," stammered the old butler, retreating toward the door.

"What about last night? Are you sure he didn't notice anything last night? Are you?"

"Positive sir," Maurice babbled, retreating toward the door, but almost ending up in the fireplace instead.

"And are you sure that Katsarida . . . ?"

"I am, sir. I am positive that he didn't see us. The garden was dark, and he was in his room. I kept an eye on his window."

"Listen," the shipowner said, sighing, "give me the address of that busybody—that *Le Clairon du Soir* journalist whose daughter is Katsarida's best friend, in spite of all my objections."

"But, Mr. Somais. Sir!"

"The address, I said! Did you hear me?" roared the Greek so vehemently that the paintings shook on the wall.

The old butler went immediately to get it.

With a heavy gait, dragging his wounded leg, the fat shipowner again walked over to the window and sighed. Above the Bois de Boulogne the sky was black. Streaks of lightning illuminated it from time to time.

"Well," Somais reflected glumly, "I always wanted my son to be an artist because I couldn't be one myself. He has no talent for painting. That can't be helped. But he picks up every single melody, even if he hears it just once. He has a marvelous ear. He could become a famous pianist. I could pay for the best teachers in the world, organize tours, bribe critics to praise him. He could be one of the world's greatest pianists! Ah, well, but what does he want? He wants to be a bicyclist, and to play that damn electric guitar! Should I leave him my millions and my magnificent ships and paintings?"

"Here's the address, master." The butler's feeble voice startled the shipowner from his reverie.

He grabbed the slip of paper from Maurice and looked at it: Marcel Cléver, Rue Erlanger 4, Paris 16, Tel: TRO 23-74. Again he frowned from the pain in his leg.

He shows his true colors   [173]

Then, suddenly he became aware that his butler was behaving very strangely. Maurice had bent over so far that his white beard almost touched the floor. Besides, he kept shifting weight from one foot to the other and looking at his master from below, like a dog who knows he's done something wrong.

"What's the matter, Maurice?" the shipowner asked, touching the butler's shoulder. "Do you feel sick?"

"I haven't told you everything, sir."

"Ah." The shipowner groaned and slumped back into his armchair. "Speak, Maurice. Speak, you wretch of a man."

The poor butler, who didn't know how to lie, related as best he could his conversation with Katsarida. The fat shipowner listened grimly to Maurice's detailed account of how Somais was being shadowed by his own son, how interested his son was in his affairs, and how suspicious he was of him. When the butler was finished, Somais said thoughtfully, "So Katsarida knows about the painter from Pelleport. Is that right?"

"If you'll forgive me, master, there's a story about the painter in the paper. It's not hard to guess," and the gray-haired butler pointed to the crumpled *Le Clairon du Soir* on the floor.

"Get out of here! Go! Vanish!" the Greek thundered, brandishing his cane in the air as if fencing with an invisible enemy.

Poor Maurice bumped against the fireplace and retreated backward out of the room as fast as he could. He remained standing by the door on the other side, knowing that his angry master would order him to come right back again.

"Damnation!" whimpered the shipowner bitterly and tottered off to the window again. The first large drops of rain started to beat against the windows.

"I won't let anyone outsmart me, oh no!" thought the Greek, looking at the sheets of rain falling over Paris. "They planted a spy in my own house. They've turned my own flesh and blood against me, smeared my name, and portrayed me as an ordinary thief. Let them! But I'll show them yet! It's not my fault that I know real art when I see it. It's not my fault that I appreciate a painting like the *Mona Lisa* more than anyone else in the world. Isn't it unfair that I, who love those paintings —love them more than my own ships—and have the money to buy them, have to fight some piddling . . ."

The shipowner turned around suddenly and yelled so loudly that once again the paintings danced on the walls.

"Maurice! Maurice!"

"Yes, sir?" the butler squeaked, tumbling into the room as fast as he could.

"Dial that number for me right away."

Then, all at once, he turned deathly pale. Dropping himself against the armchair, he stammered, "Maurice, where's the parrot? Where's our César, Maurice?"

"The master said the bird got on his nerves with his

babbling and cracking, so I put him out on the balcony."
The old butler's face was ashen. "Oh, my God! I'll go
see if he's . . . I'll run."

"Idiot!" roared the shipowner, hopping behind the
butler as fast as he could. "You left the poor precious
bird out there in that downpour. Poor César! You
blockhead! You old fool!"

When the shipowner reached the next room, he saw
the butler standing stock still at the door to the balcony.
Somais automatically assumed the worst. He thought
that poor César had drowned in the rain.

But César, though alive, and no doubt well, was not
there. Under the cage the rainwater had turned all
colors, from deep red to green. And the bird itself was
gray, the color of a common pigeon. The rain had
washed off all the colors from the bird's feathers.

"Sir," stammered the stunned butler.

"I can see for myself!" the Greek thundered. "I
thought César was behaving strangely these last few days.
Not like old César! Not at all. Give me that shaggy
sparrow!"

"But I don't understand," Maurice stuttered as he
chased the gray bird around the balcony.

"Now I understand. One more trick they've played
on me. The insurance company will pay dearly for that
joke. My César was insured for millions of francs at the
show. Give me that idiot!"

The old butler, trembling with fear, caught the bird
and handed him to the shipowner, who in turn grabbed

the bird by the neck. The poor creature fluttered its wings and cooed in mortal terror. And while it was defending itself and gasping for breath, its beak opened wide, revealing a piece of wire protruding from its throat.

"A wire!" Maurice felt positively faint.

"What the . . . ?" Somais screamed. Then, as astonished as the bird itself, he pulled a thin wire out of the beak. At the end of the wire was an instrument the size of a hazelnut. "That's a microphone, Maurice. This fake César was brought to our house so that someone could keep track of every word we say. That's the plot. But I'll show them. Maurice, call PEL 24-38."

In a few moments the butler returned to report that PEL 24-38 was not answering. The shipowner banged his cane against the floor, flung the bird to the floor, and screamed, "Bring the car around! I'm going to the painter's house myself. Personally. They baited me, and now they'll see how well I take the hook. Maurice, the car!"

This time the old butler retreated backward so fast that he stumbled and fell.

Not even Inspector Simo would be able to help

2 I Two foreign tourists, a husband and wife, were gazing out over the great city of Paris from the first landing of the Eiffel Tower.

"Oh, darling, it's wonderful here," she said and sighed with pleasure.

"Oh, darling, I'm delighted that you're delighted. I mean, I'm pleased that you're pleased, if you know what I mean."

"I know, darling. But finish taking your photographs so we can impress all our friends and relatives at home."

"Yes, darling, stand over there. That's terrific. Now say, 'Cheese.'"

The tourist aimed his expensive camera at his wife, but at that instant a cloud appeared to have covered the sun. The very next moment that cloud had dropped on his head, and having dutifully clicked the camera, the photographer fell down.

"Oh, my God!" the lady screamed, rushing to her husband's rescue.

The object that had hit the poor man was not a cloud, of course, but rather a painting wrapped in newspaper. The paper was partially torn, and the two puzzled tourists got a glimpse of the smiling face of a beautiful woman.

"Lovely woman," the wife exclaimed.

"Heavy, too," said the husband, rubbing his head.

But before the two tourists had time to reflect on what had happened, two boys shoved through the crowd, grabbed the painting away from them, and raced for the stairs.

"We've got to get away as fast as possible," Zlatko said as he desperately tried to patch up the torn paper. "Before someone realizes what we've got."

"That painting looked so familiar," said the tourist's wife. "I must have seen the woman in some movie."

"Awfully heavy," groaned the man, finally getting to his feet and thinking what a marvelous shot he must have gotten before collapsing.

Meanwhile, Koko and Zlatko had dashed down the stairs and were racing across a wide lawn in the direction of the Place du Trocadéro, unaware that they were being carefully watched by two pairs of eyes from the Café Malacoff. All they could think of was how fast they could get to the subway and from there by train to Pelleport.

In the corridors of the République station, where they were changing trains, Zlatko kept repeating, "If only I knew, if only I knew . . ."

"What? What?" Koko asked as he raced along, trying to keep up with his friend's fast pace.

"If only I knew why my uncle got mixed up in this. I just don't understand. Don't understand it at all. The most important thing is for us to return the painting. Thank God, it didn't get damaged. It could have fallen on some sharp object, you know."

"Listen, Zlatko," Koko said suddenly while they were waiting for the train. "Don't you think that friend of yours—what's his name—Simo, I mean. Don't you think he could help us?"

"Which Simo, Koko? Are you kidding?"

"You know who I mean. The man who smokes a pipe, drinks beer, and solves riddles, like who killed who—you know who I mean?"

"Ah," Zlatko remembered and was furious. "You mean Maigret. Maigret is the detective in Georges Simenon's novels, you dummy."

"I didn't know that," said Koko, crestfallen.

"I know you didn't know. You have no idea what Paris is like. Come on. Get moving."

But when they got out of the elevator at Pelleport and were on their way to Rue Bretonneau, Koko gathered together enough courage to speak again. Scratching behind his ear, he suggested that they enter the painter's apartment through the balcony, over the neighbor's roof, rather than through the main entrance of the building.

"Why?" Zlatko was puzzled but managed to conceal

Not even Inspector Simo would be able to help   [181]

it. He felt that at such tense and difficult moments no bit of advice should be rejected—if it was reasonable, of course.

"Well," said Koko hesitantly. "When the painting disappeared yesterday, temporarily I mean—I mean, now it's here and then it isn't—you know what I mean. They wanted to steal it, but were suddenly scared off. Well, which way did they come in, do you think? From the balcony? They wouldn't have dared come in through the main door."

"And then what? Suppose you're right. I still don't see the point in climbing over the roof like two idiots if we can enter the house with a key. What do we care about them?"

"What if they're in there? They don't have the key. We approach them from the back, they can't get out, and bang!"

Koko was so afraid of Zlatko's fierce reaction that by the time he had finished making his suggestion, he was whispering. Instead, his friend looked thoughtful and patted him approvingly on the back. "This time you've got a point, Koko. Let's surprise them. They've given us a hard time. Surprise is very important in any war strategy."

Koko was terribly happy as they ran up to 5 Rue Bretonneau. He was so proud of his scheme that he forgot to ask himself what would happen if indeed they found the thieves in the apartment.

The boys dashed up the stairs of the building next

door. Fortunately they didn't meet anyone. The door to the attic was unlocked. Zlatko kicked it open.

"Koko, you go in first," he said. "I can't, because I've got the painting."

Koko walked boldly into the dark attic and cautiously made his way toward a streak of light that came through a narrow opening in the roof. His heart had almost stopped beating. He climbed out through the opening and found himself on a flat roof with no railings. Forgetting his fear of heights, he was delighted to find that he had guessed correctly as to how one could get into the painter's apartment. It wouldn't be hard to jump from the roof to his uncle's balcony.

Zlatko carefully squeezed the *Mona Lisa* through the opening, then crawled out onto the roof.

"What did I tell . . . ?" Koko began triumphantly and loudly, but Zlatko smacked him across the mouth.

"Shhhh! We must be careful. We'll untie the laundry line from my uncle's balcony. Just in case we need to tie somebody up. And those loose pickets may come in handy too. You never know."

Koko was so terrified that he felt his shaggy hair standing straight up. Slowly they slipped down to the balcony, lowered the painting, and rested it against the wall. They each pulled one picket out of the rickety railing, removed the laundry line, and exchanged significant looks. They were ready. Ready for what?

From the apartment there suddenly came the piercing and persistent ringing of the doorbell.

Not even Inspector Simo would be able to help [183]

"We got here at the right moment, I think," Zlatko said.

"If, for example . . ." Koko began cautiously.

"Shut up and follow me!" Zlatko cut him short and boldly stepped into the little room that served as his uncle's workshop and from which Zlatko had taken the *Mona Lisa* the night before. The doorbell continued to ring, and the mysterious visitor was by now violently rattling the doorknob.

The mysterious visitor was none other than Alles Worson. His nerves on edge after a long drive through the dense traffic in which his enormous black limousine had barely been able to move, he was hopping up and down in front of Poklé's door, shaking the doorknob with all his strength. And his hands were powerful indeed. Who knows what would have happened to the poor painter if Worson had caught him at that moment.

"Open the door!" he growled through his teeth and his thick beard. Then he leaned his enormous body against the door. The wood crackled; the hinges groaned.

Suddenly, with a tremendous crash, the lock gave way and the door swung open. The director lost his balance and fell headlong into the room, knocking over a bottle of milk and a jug of paint brushes on his way down.

"We've got him now!" he heard a voice above him say. Hands grabbed him and pulled him and pushed him like a bunch of gruesome crabs.

Having tossed aside their pickets, which they didn't need to use as clubs, Koko and Zlatko expertly tied the bewildered director to the stairway leading up to the attic. The laundry line was very long, and they were thus able to wrap up the bearded Worson from head to toe. When they were done with him, he looked like a swaddled baby. By the time he finally came to, they had stuffed his mouth with a thick towel, and he could barely breathe.

Koko plunked the little yellow cap back on Worson's head, took a long proud look at him—the same proud feeling he had when crowning one of his snowmen with an old pot.

"There he is again," said Koko thoughtfully.

"What did you say?" Zlatko was astonished.

"Don't you realize it's the same man we saw through the binoculars from the Eiffel Tower? The one who was getting out of the helicopter? The same beard, the same glasses, the same yellow cap. It's like a dream!"

"You must be kidding! It couldn't be the same man. I think we'd better get moving. Who knows what's going on? We're done with this one, anyway."

"It's the same man, all right," Koko insisted. "Let's ask him." Koko was about to remove the towel from the director's mouth, but Zlatko rapped him on the fingers.

The telephone rang. The two boys and the actor-director stared at the black instrument, which was shaking from its own violent ringing. When the ringing stopped, Zlatko repeated, "Let's get out of here, fast."

"And leave him here like this, you mean, with the

Not even Inspector Simo would be able to help [185]

painting? Why did we come back here in the first place?"

"What are you talking about, Koko? We'll take the painting with us. And he'll be let loose. Either by his friends or by his enemies—one or the other. Ha, ha, ha." Zlatko laughed—a mean laugh. Alles Worson gave him a fierce look through his dark glasses. Koko brought the painting from the balcony and gave it to Zlatko.

"Where do we go from here, Zlatko?" he asked cautiously. "We just got here. I think . . ."

"Don't be a bore, Koko. You're not suggesting that I should tell you our plans in front of him. But I can say this much: we're going to the place where the whole mess started. We're going straight to enemy headquarters. Wait and see! You haven't the slightest notion what Paris is all about. No, you don't."

The whale has a fake beard

22 "That's right!" Marie Cléver cried happily. "Now I understand everything. It's all clear! Clear as can be. How could I have been so dumb?"

"I'll bet she doesn't understand it any more than I do. She's just showing off," Katsarida thought despondently.

The two of them stood behind a large black limousine, which was parked on Rue Bretonneau, across the street from No. 3. From their observation post at Café Malacoff they had seen the two mysterious boys recapture the *Mona Lisa,* and so Marie and Katsarida decided to follow them to the end of the world. They all ended up at the twentieth arrondissement, at Pelleport.

"It's all clear now, Katsarida, I tell you," Marie Cléver went on with her usual enthusiasm. "They're the boys who gave Poklé a sleepless night. The thieves stole the painting, the two boys followed them all over the city until finally, this morning, they snatched it back from them. Right? And now they're back in the apartment returning the painting to Poklé. Don't you see, Katsar?"

"I see, I see. But why in heaven's name did they climb to the top of the Eiffel Tower with the painting? That I don't see."

"What do you mean? What don't you see?" Marie herself was puzzled, but she hated to admit it, so she stamped her foot against the pavement. "Oh, Katsar, come on. Haven't you ever read a good spy story?"

"Of course I have, Marie."

"Well, is anything ever clear from the start? You've got to read the whole book before you can see what's what—who are the villains and who aren't. Right?"

"Right," Katsarida agreed hopelessly.

"What we have to do now is get to know the two boys and convince them they ought to cooperate with us. We may be able to help them, and they may be able to help us. Why not? They know who tried to steal the painting and why—right? Let's follow them."

Marie and Katsarida had arrived at the Pelleport station on the very same train as Zlatko and Koko. They saw the two boys entering the house at No. 5 Rue Bretonneau. After a while Marie and Katsarida followed them into the building.

"I don't understand why Poklé's name isn't on any of these doors." Katsarida was very worried indeed.

"Painters always live in attics," Marie Cléver said without hesitation.

The boy and the girl climbed up to the attic and then through the opening in the roof to the painter's balcony.

"Of course," said Marie. "A secret passage. We forgot to check on the address we have for him. For all we know the painter doesn't live here at all, but somewhere in the neighborhood."

Marie and Katsarida entered the painter's apartment just after Koko and Zlatko had left. They found themselves eye to eye with a swaddled man wearing a little yellow cap pulled down to the tops of his dark glasses. There was no trace of the boys or of the painting.

"It would be best to get out of here while . . ." Katsar began.

"Don't tell me you're scared, Katsar," the girl interrupted him. "Just as it's getting to be fabulously exciting. This gentleman here looks enough like Alles Worson to be his twin. I know Worson. I have at least a hundred photos of him. I'll bet that beard's a fake, though. Pull his beard, Katsar, and you'll see."

"I don't want to, Marie. You do it."

"Mm," the captive mumbled, wriggling his legs and arms in an attempt to free himself.

"Look," Marie shouted suddenly. "The front door is broken in. The main entrance—right?"

"Someone's coming!" Katsarida whispered, squeezing the girl's hand in terror. "Let's run!"

Indeed there was a sound of footsteps on the stairs outside.

"Let's not, Katsar," Marie Cléver replied with composure, her eyes glued to the captive creature on the floor. "Spies never run away. They retreat."

The whale has a fake beard   [189]

The green-eyed boy and the brown-haired girl retreated quickly and with dignity. First to the attic, then onto the balcony, then to the attic of the neighboring house. Their dignified retreat was closely followed by the eyes of the captive hidden behind the usual dark glasses.

A few moments later Jean Brange and Michel Croitier cautiously knocked on the wrecked door, pushed it aside, and caught sight of a large man tied to the staircase.

"Hey!" Michel cried excitedly. "Look at this! They've really wrapped him up, haven't they?"

"Didn't I tell you?" said Jean, lighting a cigarette. "I knew it would be great here."

That very morning, after the unfortunate adventure at Place d'Auteuil, Michel had gone home feeling very discouraged. He had had no idea when Jean would be released by the police, or how to explain to Jean, once he was released, how he had allowed those two Mongols to get away with the *Mona Lisa*. At the police station, Jean had merely been warned—in no uncertain terms, of course—that as a young driver he must be exceptionally careful in observing signs. They had then returned his license and let him go.

Jean immediately went to Michel's home, and the two friends decided to continue their search for the painting and for the boys who had slipped out of their hands. Michel had recalled a very important detail: the slip of paper with Zlatko's uncle's telephone number: PEL: 24-38. With that number in front of them, there was no problem finding the address. They had parked Jean's old Citroën right behind the glistening black limousine on Rue Bretonneau.

And now the two boys, who had been so anxious to visit the Loire and the Mediterranean, stood in complete astonishment in front of a man who grimly watched them from behind his dark glasses while desperately trying to free his arms and legs.

"I don't think we should untie him," Jean remarked.

"I agree, old man," Michel said. "Funny business this, which suits me fine. The messier the better."

"Could this whale be the Mongol's uncle?" Jean suggested.

"But who'd bother to tie him up? Koko and the Mongol? No. Out of the question."

The boys looked over the apartment and the little room in the attic. They poked into every corner, examined every piece of paper, knocked on every wall. No sign of the *Mona Lisa*. They went back downstairs.

"Let's ask this monstrosity here if he knows anything," Michel said. "Maybe he can tell us something."

"Remove the towel gradually," Jean suggested. "Don't try anything. sir. We just want to ask you a question."

"Mmm," mumbled the victim and jerked his leg.

Michel quickly went down on his knees, and just as he was about to remove the towel from Worson's mouth, he stepped back and yelled, "Jean, the whale has a fake beard!"

Instead of removing the towel, Michel expertly

The whale has a fake beard [191]

yanked the beard from the stranger's face. The fake beard remained partially attached to the director's cheeks, making him look more like a walrus now. Jean tossed his cigarette butt out of the window and said seriously, "Let's not get mixed up in this. I don't care what happens to him. We didn't put him here. Why should we risk our necks helping him out?"

"I agree. Who gives a damn?" Michel said casually. "He can starve to death as far as I am concerned."

"Mmm," mumbled the captive from the floor.

But Jean decided to look through his pockets anyway. In addition to cigarettes, a lighter, and a handkerchief, they also found a passport and a bunch of visiting cards.

"O-là-là!" Jean was wildly excited. He lit another cigarette. "This is Mr. Worson, the famous American director who's making a movie about the theft of the *Mona Lisa* from the Louvre. You remember? It was in the papers the other day?"

"You couldn't be more wrong!" Michel roared, his eyes narrowing to two slits. "This may be Mr. Worson's passport, but this isn't Mr. Worson. No, sir! I'll bet you Mr. Worson doesn't wear a fake beard. Reporters would have advertised that long ago. Look, old man, look at the address on these visiting cards: 23 Avenue de la Bourdonnais. Why not take a look? What do you say?"

"You're great, Michel. I'll bet you our fathers would give anything to be in our shoes right now."

"Our fathers are amateurs," Michel said angrily. "Let's

go to Avenue de la Bourdonnais, and tomorrow all Paris will have the news."

Jean shrugged, glued the beard back to the stranger's cheeks, and motioned to Michel with a firm gesture that they should clear out as fast as possible.

When they reached their old Citroën, someone kept honking impatiently behind their backs. The man wanted their space behind the large black limousine. The impatient driver was no other than the rich Greek shipowner Somais.

"Damnation!" grumbled the fat Greek while clambering up the stairs, desperately trying not to lean on his injured leg but rather on his cane. "Why is it that all artists live on the top floor of buildings without elevators?"

The old millionaire rang Poklé's doorbell for a long time. Finally, he pushed open the broken-in door and found himself face to face with the bearded captive, who was mumbling and squirming in the hopes of freeing himself.

"Well," said Somais and thumped his cane.

He looked over the entire apartment. He climbed into the attic, practically stepping over the captive's head, but found no trace either of Poklé or of the *Mona Lisa*. He paused in front of the bound man, who was still mumbling, and threatened him with his cane. "You want me to untie you, eh? I'm not mad yet. All I need at this point is another mess like this on my hands. My fin-

gerprints in this pigsty! No, sir. Good-bye. Glad to have met you. Give my regards to that painter and tell him I'll wring his neck as soon as I get my hands on him. Damnation! Look what I've been reduced to. All this for art's sake. Damnation!"

Limping and wincing from the pain in his leg, Somais tottered off through the shattered door.

Meanwhile, the poor victim with the yellow cap continued to struggle to loosen the cord around his body and to get rid of the towel in his mouth. His eyes ached with anguish.

A few minutes later a cat slinked into the room and greedily lapped up the spilt milk from the floor. After she had left, a pigeon carefully hopped onto the balcony and neatly picked up the breadcrumbs the painter had forgotten to sweep up. The victim's stomach growled like a clogged drain.

Everything's false

23 Above Boulevard de Montmorency the clouds
flitted away and the beautiful bright summer sun
emerged. Wide-eyed with admiration, Koko and Zlatko
gazed at the magnificent mansion, partly hidden by a
stone wall and several thick shaded trees.

"There are several entrances here. Which is the main
one?"

"I think I know," Zlatko said quickly. "All of the
boulevard entrances are the main entrances. That much
is clear. But we must enter from the other side. Surprise
is what counts. Let's go!"

With the painting safely tucked under his arm, Zlatko
advanced boldly alongside the stone wall, turned the
corner, and circled around the garden surrounding the
Greek shipowner's mansion.

"I'm terribly hungry," said Koko, barely able to keep
up with his friend's energetic stride. And he thought to
himself, "I'm fed up with Paris."

Before going down into the underground to get the train to the Bois de Boulogne, they had walked over to see what their friend Charles was doing: the barbershop was closed and there was no sign of anyone, which confirmed Zlatko's suspicion that the barber and his strange friend were somehow involved in the theft of the *Mona Lisa*. "Because," he reasoned further, "a real barber would keep his shop open on Saturdays. And our Charles! Ah, well, who cares? It will all be cleared up soon. My poor uncle. Why did he have to get mixed up in this?"

It comforted Zlatko to think that his uncle, whose real name was Poklepovich, was merely a tool in the hands of the Greek tycoon, who had promised him a large reward and so induced him to participate in this fraud. Besides, Zlatko felt that Somais was probably not the only person trying to take advantage of the commotion caused by the making of the film. Other people were involved as well, like the cripple, the two barbers, Michel and Jean, the man with the black beard and yellow cap, and God knows how many others—possibly all members of a gang trying to get the famous painting! "And who is going to spoil their plans, to outsmart them?" the boy thought, grinding his teeth. "Who is going to help my poor uncle get out of this dirty business? Me, of course! And Koko, maybe, if he does as he's told."

As for Koko, he was still ravenous. If only he were home now, he thought, he would agree to take a bath and drink a cup of Ovaltine, which he despised so much.

"Halt!" Zlatko hissed. He tightened his grip on the painting under his arm. "This is the back entrance to enemy headquarters. We must be extra cautious if we want to get out of here alive—and with a bit of useful information as well."

Koko scratched behind his ear and nodded. All he could think of was that glass of Ovaltine and the friendly locust tree under his window at home. He remembered the hours he had spent in his room thinking about Paris. Although Zlatko had told him many scary stories, it was still hard to believe that the two of them would spend all their time in Paris running and hiding and sneaking around.

Zlatko pushed open the garden gate and shoved Koko in ahead of him.

They walked along a narrow path that skirted the arbor and, from there, directly to the Somais mansion. Just as Koko was getting up courage to ask Zlatko what he was planing to do, they heard a piercing whistle.

"Come over here, boys!" a voice called out to them.

Before Zlatko and Koko could regain their wits, a brown-haired girl with large eyes and a whistle in her mouth and a dark-haired boy with big green eyes appeared in the deep shade of the arbor.

"Let's introduce ourselves," the girl said cheerfully, shaking her brown locks. "I'm Marie Cléver. We've been expecting you."

"I'm Katsarida," the boy said, and stuck his hand out. "Katsarida Somais."

"Oh," Zlatko said, cautiously shaking Katsarida's hand.

"Oh," Koko whined. He was desperately hungry.

"There's no point in playing games," said the future Mata Hari with a smile. "You may not know who we are, but we know all about you. And we knew you'd find us."

"I see," Zlatko said and frowned.

"I see," echoed Koko.

"His father's ruined my poor uncle," Zlatko said, pointing at Katsarida.

"That's not true!" the shipowner's son replied.

"Shut up!" Marie Cléver yelled, stamping her foot.

The girl ordered the three boys to take seats on the arbor bench, and with a finger in the air, like a school teacher, she stood in front of them.

"Now, boys, enough's enough," she said. "We're all eager to sort out this mess. And you two, Zlatko and Koko, need not be afraid of Katsar. He's in more trouble than any of us. You see, it involves his father. But let's not go into that now. We must each tell what we know about the case of the *Mona Lisa*."

Koko and Zlatko were still wary and bewildered. Katsarida cleared his throat and began carefully, "You can cut both my ears off if what I tell you now is not the truth."

And Katsarida proceeded to relate everything he knew about his father's greed for great works of art. He mentioned yesterday's statement by the old butler that the new ship would be christened the *Mona Lisa*.

"So, now, you've heard our story," Marie said. "Now we want to hear yours."

Zlatko cleared his throat. His jaws were so tightly clenched that it looked as if they might crack any minute. But he was determined to tell everything. He sensed that, here in the heart of enemy territory, he had discovered his true allies. Slowly, and in great detail, he recounted their adventures, from the time he and Koko landed at the Paris airport the day before up to this very minute.

The girl listened carefully, pencil in hand, shaking her head from time to time and jotting down the most important details. When Zlatko was through, Marie turned to Koko and asked if he had anything to contribute. Koko shrugged and said, "I'm hungry."

"No problem," said Katsarida. "I'll ask Maurice to bring us something to eat. What would you like?"

"I'd like some . . ." Koko began hesitantly and looked at Zlatko. "I don't know how to say it in French, though. I mean, I'd like some stuffed peppers."

"What did he say?" Katsarida asked.

"He would like some French fries," Zlatko said and turned to his friend in absolute disgust. "Won't you ever grow up, Koko?"

When the French fries came, twenty minutes later, the shipowner's son also brought along a gray bird whom he introduced as his former parrot, César. Then he explained to his new friends the secret of the hidden microphone that had come to light thanks to a sudden summer shower.

"The parrot!" Zlatko shouted. "That's it! The parrot and the cripple! Now everything's clear. Didn't I tell you, Koko, didn't I?"

"The cripple!" Katsarida said, so astonished that his mouth fell wide open. "I met a cripple, and he told me to follow you! There, at Place d'Auteuil! He told me you had hopped onto bus No. 52. That character knows everything, doesn't he?" He paused and then went on. "I think the cripple and the man with the beard are one and the same person," Katsarida said. "He uses different disguises so as not to attract too much attention. I'm convinced his beard is fake."

"Of course." Marie Cléver smiled. "I know Alles Worson. The man with the beard only resembles him."

"Excuse me," Zlatko suddenly interrupted, clearing his throat importantly. "Excuse me, Marie, I want to ask one question: how did you manage to get my uncle's address and telephone number last night? Your father's out of town, and there was nobody else you could ask."

Marie Cléver blushed, deeper than a true spy should. She stomped the floor bitterly and said, "That's my business. Spying is spying! It doesn't matter how I got the information."

"Marie's right," Katsarida cut in.

"Shut up, Katsar," the girl responded sharply. "The

most important thing at this point is to draw up a careful plan of action, and to do that, we must review what we know, right?"

The three boys nodded as the girl waved her notebook under their noses: "Here, see this? It's all written down here. Perk up your ears, all three of you, and if I've missed something, just yell—right? Here we go:

THE MONA LISA CASE

A film about the theft of the painting is being made. In order not to use the original during the shooting, a painter by the name of Poklé makes a new one, a perfect likeness. Poklé is an unknown painter. He wants to take advantage of the situation to become rich. He gets in touch with a rich shipowner, who adores old paintings, and particularly the *Mona Lisa*, and who has even named his new ship after it. The painter secretly exchanges the paintings, taking the original to his apartment. Why? Perhaps because he wants to exchange it again, in front of everyone, and to have the film shot with the original, while everyone thinks it is a copy. If it turns out that no one is able to tell the difference between the original and the copy, he can sell the copy for a vast sum of money to the rich shipowner, who will never know the difference. At this point some thieves enter the act—in fact, several different groups of thieves. Fake barbers plant a fake parrot with a microphone in his beak in the mansion of the rich shipowner in order to record his conversations with the painter. They try to steal the copy from the painter (not realizing it is the original!) in order to exchange it for the original at the Louvre. In this venture they are thwarted by the painter's nephew, Zlatko, and his friend, Koko. They put the painting back in its place in the attic. But the fake barbers, probably under the tutelage of the fake one-eyed cripple and the two hoodlums in the small Citroën, kidnap Koko and demand the *Mona Lisa* as ransom. Koko and Zlatko somehow manage to get away with the painting and to tie up the fake actor-director Alles Worson in the painter's apartment . . ."

"I feel sick," said Koko feebly. "I feel like throwing up."

"You think everything's fake, don't you," Zlatko said to the girl. "People and things, everything I mean. What's real?"

"*We* are real," said the girl spy proudly. "We are therefore the only ones who can solve the riddle. You'll see. Well, where were we? The fake actor director, with the fake beard . . ."

Let's go visit nobody

24 The little Citroën sneaked in between two parked cars on Rue Camou. Two boys jumped out of the car and walked over to the intersection of this narrow street and the wide Avenue de la Bourdonnais. From there they walked down the avenue to No. 23.

"Here we are," said Jean in a hollow voice, lighting a cigarette.

"I don't get it, old man," said Michel, blinking his narrow eyes. "What exactly are we doing here? Do you think we can solve the mystery of the man with the beard?"

"Look, Michel," Jean snapped, "coming here was your idea. Well, we are here now. What do you plan to do next?"

"Relax, old man, just relax," said Michel in a conciliatory tone. "Let's find out whether Worson lives here in the first place."

On the ground floor there was a glistening brass plate

with an unfamiliar name; on the floor above there was a large door with no name at all. If the famous director indeed lived there, one could only assume that he wanted to protect himself against aggressive reporters and the public.

When Jean pressed the bell, Michel's eyes watered from the tension. What if this *was* Worson's apartment? Or if Worson wasn't at home and the man with the beard, tied up in Poklé's apartment, was Worson after all? He tried to ask Jean what he thought, but Jean brushed him off impatiently and puffed out a last bit of smoke. Just as he had tossed the butt down the stairs, the door opened and Worson's secretary, with her large gold-rimmed glasses, stood in front of them, as large as life.

"Oh!" she said, surprised to see the two youngsters. "You naughty boys! How did you ever find our address? Not even the reporters can find us. You've come to get autographs—right?"

"Right you are," Jean and Michel said in chorus, pleased that they had bumped across the right door and that the secretary had provided them with an excuse as well.

"But if you were really anxious to see Mr. Worson, you should have been at the Louvre today, where he's shooting a movie right now, this very minute. He's not here, my dear boys! Sorry!"

The woman with gold-rimmed glasses was about to close the door, but Michel put out his hand, and she didn't have the heart to slam the door on his fingers.

"Lady," said Michel, "are you sure that Mr. Worson isn't sitting in the living room, drinking Coke?"

"Don't be ridiculous," answered the secretary. "I personally escorted him to the roof this morning, where he took off in a helicopter."

"Ha!" Jean interrupted. "That's just it! If he left in a helicopter, he could have come back in one."

"But he had to pass through this door anyway. Not in the helicopter, obviously, but by himself, I mean. You don't mean to suggest that he climbed in through the window."

"How about checking his room, huh? Just a peek, won't you, please?" Michel insisted.

The secretary led them down a long corridor.

"All right, boys, I'll show you his workroom. I'll give each of you one of his photographs, and you'll see for yourselves that he isn't home. Here!"

The two boys ran along the parquet floor and paused, one on each side of the secretary, in front of a door. Briskly pressing the gold knob, she swung open the heavy door.

"Oooh!" All three of them gasped and staggered backward.

A yellow cap on his head, a bottle of Coke in his hand, the famous actor-director was sitting in the middle of a luxuriously furnished room. From behind his dark glasses he cast ferocious looks at them.

"What is this?" he roared. "This is beyond belief!

Let's go visit nobody [207]

Linda! *Linda!* How dare you barge in with these two young idiots? Have you gone mad, Linda?"

"Sir . . . Mr. Worson," stammered the poor secretary. "I didn't know, I honestly didn't know. I saw you off myself from the roof this morning. I was sure you hadn't returned, and I still don't understand a thing. You've simply got to believe me! Please!"

"Who are these two guys?" roared the director.

"I don't know. I haven't any idea," mumbled Linda.

Jean Brange and Michel Croitier bowed from the waist down and humbly introduced themselves, assuming that their names would mean nothing to the great director.

"You lunatic snoopers!" Worson howled as Coke spilled all over the thick carpet. "How did you find out where I live?"

"From your double," said Jean, after he had collected himself a bit. And then he added, "Either he's your double, or you're his."

In an instant, in three swift leaps, Michel bounded up to Worson, pulled his beard, and exclaimed cheerfully, "This is the real one! The one who's tied up to the stairs is his double!"

The woman with the gold-rimmed glasses and the man with the yellow cap stared at each other in absolute astonishment. Alles Worson roared again, "What double, you idiots? What are you talking about?"

Worson was momentarily stunned. He quickly recovered, however. Plunking the Coke bottle down on the table, he bent over, grabbed his stomach, and began to laugh so loudly that the bottle danced on the table.

"Tied to the stairs, did you say? Ha, ha, ha! If someone had put the *Mona Lisa* on the wall above him, it would be identical to the scene we are going to shoot tomorrow! You remember, Linda, when the Italian, who stole the painting from the Louvre, ties his friend up under the *Mona Lisa* and practically lets him perish of hunger. And now he . . ."

"Who's he?" asked Michel.

"He?" Worson enigmatically repeated the question and suddenly grew thoughtful. Then he roared again so loudly that the Coke bottle tumbled off the table and onto the floor. "Out! Linda! Toss them out! I've had it. I'm not going to account . . ."

Jean and Michel retreated toward the door as fast as they could, and Linda followed, her arms outstretched, as if chasing chickens in the barnyard. But when they reached the main door, a fresh howl reached them from Worson's room, "Stop! Bring them back, Linda!"

Confused and terrified, Jean and Michel returned. They had had enough adventure and were willing to forget their passionate desire for revenge. By now they were quite willing to give up their trips to the Loire and the Riviera in exchange for a quiet return to their homes without Worson and without the *Mona Lisa*, to be left alone to watch the play-off match between Reims and Nantes on television.

"Who sent you here?" asked the director, removing

his dark glasses for once. "Who sent you to see me?"

"Who?" the boys sounded surprised. "Who? Nobody."

"Nobody, you say? Do you? Fine, then. Let's go visit that nobody."

"What did you say?" Jean was flabbergasted.

"This guy's lost his mind," Michel whispered, his eyes narrowing to slits.

"Linda!" the director screamed and put his glasses back on. "Telephone for the helicopter right away! Enough's enough! I'm not going to let anyone make a fool of me. No! Not any longer! Get ready, boys. Let's go visit nobody!"

Where's the original painting?

25 "You remember what it was like when we launched the *Cleopatra*? Father just barely saved his skin. And now it's the *Mona Lisa*. Oh, well, it's all clear now! Clear as can be, my dear Maurice. That's why he's so bad-tempered. Crack!"

"What does 'crack' mean, Frédéric?" Charles asked and turned off the tape recorder, cutting off Katsarida's voice.

"That's the sound I sometimes hear when I turn off the recorder and turn on the speaker. When they were talking too softly or when they got too far away from the parrot, I'd plug in the speaker and screech, 'Louder! Clearer! Good night!' or something along those lines."

"You're mad, Frédéric. You really are."

"Why, Charles? César's actually a very clever parrot who can say all kinds of things. And I didn't want them to be suspicious about the new parrot. They would have found it strange if he'd suddenly stopped talking."

"Good! Keep going," Charles said, wrinkling his nose and turning on the tape again. He waited impatiently for the end of Katsarida's conversation with Maurice. He wanted to hear the telephone conversation with Poklé and the one with Koko's mysterious deep-voiced kidnapper, who mistook Katsarida for his father and offered to sell him the *Mona Lisa*.

"We've heard that one a hundred times," said Frédéric, disgruntled. "Maybe we'll hear something new. Never can tell."

And they did.

The tape turned silently for a while. Then there was the creak of a heavy door mixed with the sound of approaching footsteps. Finally, the voice of the old butler, Maurice, filled the barbershop.

"Sir."

"I can see for myself," thundered Somais. "I thought César was behaving strangely these last few days. Not like old César! Not at all! Give me that shaggy sparrow!"

"Au!" screamed Frédéric.

"But I don't understand," stuttered old Maurice.

"But I understand," continued the Greek. "One more trick they've played on me. The insurance company will pay dearly for that joke. My César was insured for millions of francs at the show. Give me that idiot!"

"A wire," Maurice gasped.

"What the . . . ?" Somais screamed. "That's a microphone, Maurice . . ."

The shipowner had pulled the tiny microphone out of the bird's beak, which brought to an end the recorded sound on Charles and Frédéric's tape recorder. The two barbers sadly watched as the tape continued to turn, silently and monotonously.

" 'One more trick they've played on me.' 'They,' that's us," Frédéric stammered.

"I'm afraid you're right, Charles."

"No use complaining, I suppose. In our business you've got to take risks."

"That's what I always say," Frédéric agreed readily, his black moustache drooping. "All the same, what do we do now? How can we find out what that mad tycoon plans to do next?"

"Don't talk that way, Frédéric," Charles said, frowning. "Talk, talk, talk, like a windmill. Take the tape recorder away. I don't want to look at it. Let me collect myself. You're more boring than my son Michel. 'What do we do, what do we do?' We'll think of something. The game isn't lost yet. Blabbering never did anyone any good. Don't you ever get tired of the sound of your voice? No one can get a word in, for heaven's sake."

And so Charles went on and on about how one shouldn't talk too much. Frédéric listened with his head sadly lowered.

"What should we do with the man with the beard?" Frédéric finally ventured.

"I don't give a damn about the man with the beard!" Charles snapped back.

Where's the original painting? [213]

A few minutes earlier, the two barbers, like so many other people that day, had dropped in at Poklé's apartment on Rue Bretonneau. They had sneaked into the attic through the neighboring balcony and, to their great sorrow, had discovered in their turn that the *Mona Lisa* was not there. To their surprise, however, they had found someone tied to the stairs—someone who, from the back anyway, resembled the actor-director Worson. They had left the apartment as fast as their legs would carry them, across the balcony and the roof, and down the stairs of the neighboring house. They hadn't wanted to get entangled in the mysteries of the man with a fake beard. They had enough worries of their own.

"And it all began so well," said Frédéric with a sigh.

"Yes. We kept our eyes on them—and our ears too, you might say," Charles agreed, wrinkling his nose. "And our idea about the painting was terrific. With our excellent connections at the Louvre we managed to bring off the impossible: We actually did get hold of the original painting! Of course, that little fool had to nearly catch us red-handed while his friend was taking a shower! Nevertheless, we actually had the real *Mona Lisa* hanging in the painter's attic! If Paris only knew that! If only the *world* knew! Oh, dear God! Why did we do it, Frédéric? Today—think of it—today was the day they exchanged the painting at the Louvre. They thought they were exchanging the fake one for the original. But we had it planned the other way around. Which meant they would have shot the movie with the original *Mona Lisa,* which wouldn't have done it any harm, actually. And we would have kept an eye on it anyway. As for the other one, which everyone thought was the original, we didn't give a damn what happened to it. But look what happened, Frédéric! The original disappeared. We were outsmarted by a bunch of operators more clever than we are. More clever except they think they have the fake and that they'll be able to replace it with the real one. Don't you see, Frédéric? That's our last hope. Otherwise, well . . ."

And so the two barbers, Charles and Frédéric, sat there, staring dully out at the Paris traffic through the curtains of their shopwindow.

"You know, Frédéric, I'm still mad that when we dressed as the old couple and followed Poklé and the girl from the Louvre, as you suggested, we let that little brat get the better of us. It was a ridiculous idea."

"Not nearly as ridiculous as your idea of starting barbershops! If we'd dressed up like street cleaners, as I suggested, we would have been much better off. We could have hung around Poklé's apartment house and the Greek's house for as long as we wanted and whenever we wanted. Nobody would have suspected us. This way I have to watch for the Greek's car and for the crazy painter from his shop here until my eyes ache!"

"But you can't go on cleaning the street forever, Frédéric, now can you? People know there's something fishy going on if they see a man cleaning the same street over and over. Now have some sense!"

Where's the original painting? [215]

"Still, that would have been better than cutting an innocent man's throat and ending up in jail for life. You were wrong. You don't learn to be a barber by attending a ten-day training course. That's not all there is to it. My hands shake like crazy every time somebody sits down in the chair. And I feel bad that Jean and I haven't gone to the Loire. I promised him, you know."

"And what about me? I promised Michel I'd take him to the coast. I made the same promise last year, and I never kept it . . ."

"Business is business, Charles. There's nothing I can do about that!" Frédéric sighed, running his fingers through his moustache.

As the two stared out the window, neither realized that it was Saturday—the busiest day for Paris barbers. Charles walked to the back of the shop to feed hemp seed to the real César. Then he returned, slumped down into his chair, and said, "I felt much better last year when we were firemen. Even though you almost fell off the roof and I almost fell down the chimney, even so . . ."

"Charles!" Frédéric suddenly screamed and leaped to his feet. "He passed by, Charles, I swear!"

"Who? Who, Frédéric? Calm down! Easy does it."

"He! Our Greek! In a car!"

Without another word and without a single glance back at the barbershop, Frédéric and Charles rushed into the street and jumped into their dark red car, the very same car Koko had spotted the day before from the painter's balcony. And now that car was speeding furiously through the Paris traffic, following Somais's black limousine.

They didn't get very far, though.

At the first newspaper stand, the Greek brought his limousine to a sudden stop (in spite of the infernal sound of horns angrily tooting behind him), clambered out, picked up a newspaper, and quickly got back in behind the steering wheel.

"*Le Clairon du Soir!*" Frédéric cried out as he watched this scene. "How could we have forgotten it? Especially after yesterday? These damn reporters get on the track fast."

"Never mind," Charles said, wrinkling his nose again. "Who cares about *Le Clairon?* Just drive carefully and make sure we don't lose sight of the Greek. We must find out where he's going. There's hope for us now, Frédéric, I'm telling you."

Dripping with sweat, Frédéric managed to get right behind the Greek and was now tailing him. They could see the Greek nervously reading the paper he had just bought whenever he stopped for a red light.

"If only I could find out what the paper says," Frédéric mused aloud, keeping an eye on the large limousine.

Charles was about to say something, but he didn't

get a chance. Frédéric's wish to read the evening paper came true much faster than he had hoped—and very unpleasantly.

As the long line of cars moved from the corner of Rue de Rivoli in the direction of Place de la Concorde, the fat shipowner opened the window and angrily tossed out his copy of *Le Clairon du Soir*. Picked up by a gust of wind, it fluttered toward the dark red Peugeot driven by the two barbers, then spread out like a huge butterfly on the car's windshield.

Frédéric, unable to see a thing, slammed his foot on the brake. At least twenty cars also came to a sudden

stop, and somewhere behind the Peugeot, there was a crash. The pursuers of the Greek shipowner Somais jerked forward. And as Charles's nose banged against the windshield, Charles caught sight of a huge headline that read: WHERE'S THE ORIGINAL MONA LISA?

Under this headline, the article began:

Le Clairon du Soir brings to its readers the story of the mysterious paths of the famous painting, which—unbeknownst to the general public, and least of all to the administration of the Louvre—has recently been roaming the streets of Paris.

26 "I found the painter's address in my father's pocket," said Marie, blushing. "If you really want to know. . . . Well, when my father goes away, our cat Leo is frantic, you know. He goes all over the house looking for things that smell of my father. He knocked over a chair—right?—with my father's coat on it. His cigarettes fell out and a few slips of paper. One had the painter's address and phone number in large letters."

"You don't have to apologize," Zlatko said seriously. "I just asked. I was simply interested in knowing how you managed to get my uncle's address so fast. What you are telling me now is that your father had known him before."

"I said nothing of the kind," said the girl.

"What do we do now?" Koko interjected suddenly.

"Shut up, Koko," Zlatko barked, casting an angry

glance at his friend whose mouth was still greasy from the French fries he had eaten.

The three boys and the girl were sitting in the arbor. It was getting dark. Marie Cléver walked over to ask Maurice to telephone her home to find out if her father had returned from his trip, but the door to the Somais mansion was locked. She decided to go home to Rue Erlanger and find out what was going on. While she was away, the three boys went over the *Mona Lisa* affair in minute detail. Each had his own theory.

Zlatko believed that in order to make a fortune for himself, his uncle had tried to get a hold of the painting for the shipowner.

Katsarida assumed that his father had initiated the deal by offering Poklé a vast sum of money to exchange his copy of the *Mona Lisa* for the original at the Louvre.

To the absolute astonishment of Zlatko and Katsarida, Koko announced that neither Somais nor Poklé was the guilty one, but rather the gangsters who had organized his kidnapping. In Koko's opinion, these gangsters, acting under orders from the cripple, had sent Jean and Michel to kidnap him and to get the painting, knowing that suspicion would automatically fall on the shipowner and the painter rather than on them.

Then Marie came back—entirely out of breath, of course—and told them that her father had not yet returned, and that the *Le Clairon du Soir* was constantly phoning the house to find out where he was.

"Still and all, I don't understand," Zlatko continued, his jaws tense. "I still don't understand how my uncle's address got into your father's pocket."

"Why? What's so unusual about that?" Marie asked. "My father's a reporter. Why shouldn't he have his address?"

"But who could have given it to him? My uncle's name was a secret. The only one who had it was Worson. Could Worson have given it to your father?"

"Worson never saw him. My father wanted to talk to him the night before the filming started, but Worson wouldn't see him even though they were friends."

"It's that gang, I'm telling you!" Koko interjected.

"Koko!" Zlatko said sternly. Then in a gentler voice, he asked Marie, "Did you say that your father and Worson are friends? Now I'm beginning to understand it all."

But Marie Cléver didn't get a chance to answer. Footsteps sounded on the pebbled path that led from the arbor to the house. Through the thick foliage they could see the frantic face of the old butler, Maurice.

"Come here quickly, Master Katsarida," said the butler, stroking his white beard. "Look! It's a disaster!"

The young Greek took the newspaper from the old man's trembling hand. His large green eyes widened with excitement. It was the last edition of the paper, still smelling of fresh ink.

Zlatko read aloud over Katsarida's shoulder:

Le Clairon du Soir brings to its readers the story of the mysterious paths of the famous painting, which—unbeknownst to the general public, and least of all to the administration of the Louvre—has recently been roaming the streets of Paris.

As we reported yesterday, a film is being made in Paris about the most valuable painting in the world, Leonardo's *Mona Lisa*, which was stolen from the Louvre after World War I by a demented Italian patriot. Far-reaching precautions have been taken to prevent a theft during the shooting. For this purpose an unknown painter made a superb reproduction, for use in the film itself.

But before the shooting ever started, however, the unknown painter substituted his copy for the original, smuggling the original out of the Louvre and to his own apartment. It has been speculated that this plan was concocted by a wealthy collector interested in acquiring the precious painting. Presumably he paid the painter to make the substitution. It is a curious coincidence that at this very moment in the Greek shipyards a gigantic transatlantic ship is being completed that will be christened, as we have learned from reliable sources, the *Mona Lisa*.

But this is not where the story ends. Another gang of thieves—unless it is one and the same gang—with the help of a mysterious cripple, two boys and two barbers, have stolen the work of art from the painter's apartment, not realizing that what they had in their possession was the original! The painter's nephew managed to retrieve the true painting from the thieves and with a friend (both are minors) now roams the streets of Paris with this incredible treasure tucked under his arm.

Where is the real *Mona Lisa* now? The last time we saw

it, believe it or not, was when the boys accidentally dropped it from the Eiffel Tower. Millions and millions of francs flew through the air.

Tomorrow we will bring you more news of the extraordinary adventures of the *Mona Lisa,* which is being exclusively followed through the streets of Paris by your *Le Clairon du Soir* reporter. Don't forget to get your copy tomorrow, featuring the next installment in the greatest hoax and theft of the century.

Marcel Cléver

"How did your father find out so much? Even the name of the ship?" Katsarida exclaimed in complete astonishment.

"Sensational!" said Zlatko, grinding his teeth.

"I really don't understand," said Marie, blushing.

Koko thought it best not to say anything. He still didn't have the courage of his convictions. He was not staring at the paper, like the rest of them. Instead, he was watching the old butler. Maurice's hunched figure, his long white beard, and hooked nose were so familiar. Koko felt he had seen him somewhere before. Suddenly, the butler stepped back in terror. The garden gate was opening. Koko screamed.

"Someone's coming!"

It was the great boss himself—Somais. Banging his cane furiously against the pebbled path, the Greek was walking as fast as his legs would carry him. He was cursing at the top of his lungs, "Damnation! Damnation!"

The butler was retreating, followed by his master. The four in the arbor exchanged silent looks.

"My father's angry as a lion!" whispered Katsarida.

"He must have read the piece in *Le Clairon du Soir*," whispered Marie Cléver, smiling slyly with her gray eyes.

"I really don't understand, if he was out of Paris, how your father managed to write this article. With all those details too," answered Zlatko.

"Someone else is coming!" Koko whispered.

Just as the old butler was backing into the house, followed by the fuming shipowner, the garden gate opened again.

"The barber!" Zlatko gasped.

"Two barbers!" Koko corrected him and scratched behind his ear.

At first they only saw the broad nose announcing Charles Croitier, the barber from Avenue Gambetta. A split second later they saw the black moustache of Frédéric Brange, the barber from Place d'Auteuil.

"I'll have both my ears cut off if . . ." Katsarida began.

"Shhhh," hissed the girl and raised her foot as if to stomp the pavement with it, but managed to control the impulse.

"Let's go after them," Zlatko said through tight lips.

"Let's stay alive," Koko thought and sighed.

And so, shortly after Maurice and his master walked into the house through the back door, two suspicious barbers, Frédéric and Charles, were slowly and quietly ascending the main stairs.

They were, in turn, followed by Marie Cléver, whose model was the famous spy Mata Hari, by Katsarida Somais, the green-eyed boy whose great passion was to become a bicycle champion, by Zlatko, tense and curious, striding noiselessly, the painting under his arm, looking back to make sure Koko was still there, and by Koko, who was thinking nostalgically about the locust tree under his bedroom window.

Former fake cripple

27 A thin man, his hair ridiculously cropped and his beard shorn and scraggy, sat alone, in front of his thirteenth glass of wine. He was puffing away on a pipe. From time to time he would reach for his beard and run his hand over his cheek instead. Whenever the owner of the café on Place Paul-Signac noticed that his guest's glass was empty, he would leap up and fill it.

"Oh, God," Poklé groaned disconsolately. "Oh, my God."

"Do you feel bad, sir?" the café owner asked sympathetically.

"Bad? What? I'm dying, my dear friend. In fact, I'm a corpse. I might just as well have dropped from the Eiffel Tower. I've been waiting for this for thirteen years, and now that it's here—flop!"

"Flop, sir?"

"Listen, friend," the painter continued, bringing the thirteenth glass of wine to his lips, "have you ever been the happiest man in the world one day and the saddest man in the world the next? One day you are in seventh heaven, and the next, say, in the seventh circle of hell? Has that sort of thing ever happened to you?"

"Of course, sir," said the café owner and bowed courteously. "For example, sir, once I won thirteen thousand new francs on the lottery, and when I ran home to give my wife the happy news, I slipped and broke my leg. The café was closed for seven weeks, seven long weeks, so that I ended up losing more than I won."

"Ah, my dear man, that's . . ." Poklé began thoughtfully, "My dear man . . ."

"Yes, sir?" the café owner said expectantly, but decided that his guest must be drunk after all.

At that very moment a shadow fell over the table. The painter and the café owner turned their heads in surprise.

Before them stood a man with a wooden leg and a black patch over his eye. He bowed and smiled kindly.

"What can I do for you, sir?" the café owner asked pleasantly.

"I'd like to talk to Mr. Poklé privately," said the cripple. "Provided he has no objections, of course."

"I don't know you," said the painter. He was tired and cross. "And I won't talk to you, and that's that."

"You're making a mistake, Poklé," the cripple went on, calmly but persistently. "It's not true that we don't know one another. Yesterday you were out of matches, and I gave you one. Here, look, you've still got them."

"Take your matches and get lost! You sent me to that barber who ruined my head. Look at me! A disaster, that's what it is."

"I wanted to talk with you yesterday, but you refused," the cripple replied, not at all put off. "And I could have spared you a lot of trouble. I knew where your painting was, and I wanted to help."

The painter jumped up from his chair with such force that he almost turned the table over. He swayed and gave the cripple a dazed look.

"So I thought, of course," said the cripple calmly, "that if you'd hear me out, you might feel better."

"Of course, of course!" Poklé said feverishly, swaying back and forth on his feet, the thirteen glasses of red wine coursing through his blood. "Now. Now. Right now."

"It would be better if we could go elsewhere if you don't mind. Much too public . . ."

"If it would be the gentlemen's pleasure," the café owner said kindly, "I have a little room in the back, for special guests, shall I say? Complete privacy."

"But I'm waiting for someone," Poklé remembered and reached for his beard again. "I've got to stay here."

"Out of the question," the cripple said with a smile. "Anyway, little Marie couldn't possibly get here that fast. Right now she's got other things on her mind."

The poor painter was now deathly pale. He gazed with complete astonishment at this man, about whom he knew nothing but who clearly knew everything

Former fake cripple [231]

about him. "I'm done for. They've caught up with me," he thought. "I should have gone to the Eiffel Tower right away. I would have been better off."

The cripple took Poklé's arm gently, and the two men followed the café owner. A few moments later they were in a little room at the other end of the café. The painter ordered two glasses of wine. The waiter brought the wine and left. The cripple locked the door behind him.

"Here we go!" thought Poklé. "This is the beginning."

"I can't take it any more!" said the cripple. "Forgive me."

To the painter's astonishment, the stranger sat down and, leaning over, began to work on his wooden leg. He untied the strings, undid the buckles, and—removed the wooden leg! Then he quickly lowered his wide trouser leg, straightened out his knee and his real healthy left leg appeared under the table. He got up, put his wooden leg in the corner, and good-naturedly walked up and down the room to exercise his left leg, which must have gone to sleep in that unnatural position.

"It's terrible to put up with this kind of thing for so long," he said cheerfully. "I couldn't wait to take it off!"

"You! You!" Poklé stammered, still not taking his eyes off the wooden leg in the corner. "You aren't a cripple at all!"

"I'm a writer," the stranger replied and sat down at

the table again. "Forgive me for not having introduced myself. Just a moment!" and he ripped the black patch off from his right eye. Poklé almost collapsed.

Two smiling healthy eyes were now staring at Poklé. The fake cripple raised his glass, clinked the painter's fourteenth glass with it, and bowed courteously, "I am Ivan Kušan. Ivan Kušan, the writer."

"I am Poklé. Pleased to meet you," said the bewildered painter, unaware that they had stopped speaking French.

"You don't have to say any more, I know you well. You used to be a tenant at the Kosichs in Zagreb. At Melita's. I know them very well," the fake cripple began. "But I know you from Paris as well. You are one of the heroes of my new novel about the theft of the *Mona Lisa.*"

"Me?" Poklé was wide-eyed. He burped for good measure. "I can't be a hero! Only a coward. I've never been a hero. You just don't know me. I'm even afraid of dogs—did you know that?"

"Yes, I did," the writer said and smiled. "But that's of no consequence now. What is important is that you realize that I'm no burglar. I'm your friend. I feel badly about having upset you so much in my novel. I'm grateful to you, though, for having helped me make this story so exciting."

And Ivan Kušan continued with his astonishing story —about how he had advised Dr. Perich to send his son Zlatko and his best friend Koko to Paris for the summer.

Former fake cripple [233]

Kušan had to write a new book on the adventures of Zlatko and Koko, but at home nothing was happening. They went to school, did their homework, played football—in short they lived like hundreds of thousands of boys their age. No adventures in sight! So Kušan thought of sending them to a metropolis like Paris, where they might experience something very special. And he was right, of course.

"Except, you know," said Kušan, smiling, "although I understood that there'd be a lot of confusion about the *Mona Lisa*, the story was not going well. So I had to get involved personally, to make sure I got a novel out of it. I got hold of this wooden leg, you see, and put a black patch on my eye. I became the most mysterious character in my own book.

"Oh," said Poklepovich with a sigh. Could he be talking to a madman?

The writer described in great detail how, in the last two days, disguised as a cripple, he had cropped up at crucial times to divert the course of events into the most suitable direction. For example, he had given the awkward barber Frédéric the copy of *Le Clairon du Soir* to call his attention to the interesting article on the theft of the *Mona Lisa*. He had stood at the corner of Rue Bretonneau and Rue Pelleport until Koko spotted him, rushed out of the house, and got lost in the strange city. He had given matches to the painter and urged him to have a haircut at Charles's. He had suggested to Jean and Michel that they kidnap Koko; and at the entrance to Rue d'Auteuil he had removed the one-way street sign to prevent a premature meeting of Koko's kidnappers with the son of the Greek shipowner. He was also the man who whispered in Katsarida's ear the number of the bus Koko and Zlatko had taken to the Trocadéro.

"The most difficult moment was standing there while the *Mona Lisa* dropped from the top of the Eiffel Tower," concluded the author with a smile.

"Oh, God," the unhappy painter wheezed. "I didn't know! It fell from the Eiffel Tower! I'm finished. You know! You know everything! I don't even have to tell you."

"Please, don't get excited," Kušan said, holding out his glass of wine to the excited painter. "I'm apologizing to you. Indeed I'm sorry that you had to fret so much, but I assure you the painting the boys dragged all over Paris is not the real one."

"Ah," exclaimed Poklé. "If only you were right, my dear man! Oh, God! But you're altogether wrong. The painting *is* the real one. Listen to me . . ."

Stammering and hiccupping, the painter told the story about how he had managed to substitute his own *Mona Lisa* for the real one at the Louvre. His plan of action was simple. When the rich shipowner began to inquire about his copy of the *Mona Lisa*, Poklé decided to exchange the painting ahead of time. When the shooting began, in front of numerous witnesses including Worson, the director, he would take down his copy, which everyone believed was the original, and hang up the Leonardo, which everyone would then take to be his copy. When it became known that the original had been used in the film, there would be quite a stir, but the value of his painting would increase tenfold. For it would become generally known that Poklé's work was indistinguishable from Leonardo's masterpiece.

And then the original disappeared from the attic on Rue Bretonneau! What else could the poor painter expect but several years in prison? All his ships sank at once, and the only solution was the Eiffel Tower.

"Nonsense," exclaimed the former fake cripple cheerfully. "You are wrong. The painting that fell from the Eiffel Tower was not yours. The two barbers, Charles and Frédéric, got into the act and exchanged the paintings once again! Give me those matches—yes, those I gave you yesterday. I'll explain it to you with matches. It's hard to explain everything with words."

The writer took the matchbox and carefully tore it in half.

"Let's say this half is the original *Mona Lisa*," said Kušan. He wrote ORIGINAL on it. "And the other half is the fake, if you'll forgive the expression." And he wrote FAKE. "Now, look carefully!"

And the writer placed the two halves on the table.

"And who are those two barbers anyway," asked the rattled painter, "and why would they be doing me a favor?"

"You a favor? Nonsense. They were thinking only

of themselves. They had no idea, you understand, that the original was in your apartment. They thought they were taking your painting to the Louvre."

"Oh. Your novel sounds much too complicated." Poklé sighed. "And what would have happened if I had jumped off the Eiffel Tower?"

"I would never have allowed that to happen. I would have been right next to you, and I would have grabbed your hand. Or your leg, if necessary. Besides, I wasn't the one who made the story much too complicated! The person who got the story tied up in knots is literally tied up in knots in your apartment. It's time we visited him.

"Waiter, check, please!" shouted the former fake cripple.

Everyone against everyone

2 8 Shaking like a leaf, Maurice, the old butler, had planted himself between his master and his enemies. The shipowners peeked from behind Maurice's shoulders, waved his cane, and shouted, "Damnation! Who are you two? What do you want from me?"

"Get out, or we'll call the police," the old butler said boldly.

"Police? Ha, ha," Charles laughed bitterly. "I'd sure like to see that. If anyone is afraid of the police, it sure isn't us. We've got it all down, all of it taped down to the last word, your complete conversation with that scoundrel Poklé. You'd be better off just telling us where the painting is before we call the police."

"Painting?" roared the shipowner, whacking the wall with his cane. "So *that's* what you want? You're looking for the *Mona Lisa*. You are the people who stole my parrot, you . . ."

"Don't get so excited, sir. Your leg will act up again," Maurice said, trying to calm his master.

"Yes, sir." Charles was firm now. "We are looking for the *Mona Lisa*. We are not only looking for it, but we are going to find it. Here, in this house!"

"Damnation!" Somais shouted. "Get out!"

Then suddenly came the calm voice of a tall, thin boy whose head was shaved like a Mongol's.

"The painting's here," the boy said.

"Don't get all upset. We'll explain everything," said Marie Cléver and smiled with her large gray eyes.

"Calm down, Father. It's not your fault," Katsarida said, walking over to his father.

"For example . . ." Koko began, but he didn't know how to continue.

The grownups looked in great surprise at the young foursome. No one seemed to know what was going on. Only Maurice was smiling.

Marie Cléver rattled off everything she knew in connection with the mysterious events surrounding the two *Mona Lisas*. Little by little the assembled group began to understand what had happened in the past twenty-four hours. Fathers Frédéric and Charles explained that they had exchanged the painting, which had already been exchanged, and that therefore the one that had fallen from the Eiffel Tower and that Zlatko was holding under his arm was not the original *Mona Lisa* but Poklé's copy. At that point Zlatko put the painting down, resting it against the wall. Up to then, "just in case," he had been holding it so firmly under his arm that his fingers were numb.

Meanwhile, the fat shipowner collapsed into his arm-chair. The painful throbbing in his leg subsided. He began his story.

"I can hardly tell you," he said slowly, but with obvious pleasure, "how happy I am that my tortures have come to an end. Raphael's *Cleopatra* disappeared, and I gave my ship the same name. It was a complete accident. The newspapers were suspicious, of course, because of my art collection. Again, as ill luck would have it, just as I decided to christen my new ship after Leonardo's most famous painting, the shooting of a movie about the theft of the *Mona Lisa* began in Paris!"

"Father!" Katsarida said, jumping up with excitement, his green eyes shining triumphantly as if he had just won the Tour de France. "But, why then, at the time when the *Cleopatra* disappeared, while we were on our way from New York to Greece, did you lock yourself into your cabin every night and refuse to let anyone in? I'll bet you had . . ."

"Tell him, Maurice. Tell him the truth," Somais said in a tired voice.

"Mr. Somais went into his cabin every night to paint his own works—mostly fishes. And he didn't wish to be observed or disturbed," the old butler said and bowed.

"Father," Katsarida said, obviously not satisfied with this reply. "Explain one more thing! Last night, you and Maurice carried into the house a flat object wrapped up in . . ."

Everyone against everyone [241]

"Tell him, Maurice," interrupted Somais impatiently.

"That was supposed to be a surprise for your fifteenth birthday, young master. Mr. Somais bought you an electric guitar," Maurice explained happily.

Marie Cléver clapped her hands so enthusiastically that her brown locks danced about her head, and Katsarida lowered his head in shame. Just then the door sprang open and in burst a large man with a black beard and a yellow cap above his dark glasses. It was none other than Alles Worson.

"That's him!" Marie exclaimed ecstatically and dashed toward the new guest. "Can't you see that he's different from the one who's tied up!"

"Humbug!" thundered Alles Worson. "Humbug! I'm here to settle accounts, Mr. Somais. A friend of mine asked me to help lay a trap to expose you. The way I see it, though, you managed to trap him and get the painting into the bargain."

"Mr. Worson," Marie Cléver said, grabbing his hand excitedly, "we'll explain everything."

"I don't want any more explanations," Worson said, flailing his arms. "You even dared to send spies to my apartment. They're here now, those two rascals!"

Everyone turned to follow the director's finger, which was pointing to the door.

"My son!" exclaimed Frédéric.

"Michel!" Charles cried out in astonishment.

"Perhaps you two boys will be able to explain to us

who your fathers are," Zlatko said, "and why they should be posing like barbers and ravaging everyone within reach."

"Barbers! Ha, ha, ha!" Jean burst into loud laughter.

"What did I tell you, Jean?" Michel said with a smile. "And they fixed up the Mongol. Just look at him!"

"Barbers did you say, Zlatko?" Jean asked, suddenly serious. "Of course, they aren't barbers. Our fathers work for an insurance company. The Louvre has probably insured the *Mona Lisa* for some enormous sum of money against theft or damage. If an insurance man prevents damage or loss of an insured object, he gets a handsome reward. Last year they disguised themselves as firemen in order to keep an eye on an English lord's jewels, and they almost lost their lives."

"The cops grabbed them and tossed them into jail," said Michel.

"And the agreement was that if they'd managed to win the reward," Jean continued, lighting a cigarette, which he would not ordinarily have had the courage to do in front of his father, "Michel would get a trip to the Riviera and I a trip to the Loire. They've been promising us those trips for three years now."

The fake barbers, their eyes glued to the thick rug on the drawing room floor, were wondering what the insurance must be on a wealthy home like this. The host banged his cane against the rug and roared, "Now I understand it all! How they got hold of my parrot, my

César! I insured him for the show, and they must be from my insurance company. They planted that ridiculous scavenger . . ."

"César's alive and happy," Charles said.

"We fed him hens, I mean hemp," Frédéric blabbed.

Before the Greek was able to respond, a new person appeared at the door. In front of the assemblage stood none other than the famous reporter for *Le Clairon du Soir*, Marcel Cléver, his hair strangely cropped, his face lined with scratches.

"Papa!" exclaimed Marie, running to her father. "You've come back, after all. I thought, you see . . ."

"Let's leave that until later, Marie," the reporter said, "when I'll have some questions to ask you, too. First, I must apologize to some of those present here. I am Marcel Cléver, the reporter for *Le Clairon du Soir*, which played a somewhat ignominious role in the humorous events surrounding the *Mona Lisa*, both the original and the fake . . ."

"Damnation!" Somais roared, clutching his leg, which was obviously acting up again. "Maurice, throw this cad out!"

"Don't do that, Mr. Somais," Alles Worson said. "He's a friend of mine, and I'm sure he'll be able to explain what caused this whole misunderstanding."

"I'll certainly try," the reporter went on. "You've heard the rumor going around Paris to the effect that certain wealthy people are eager to obtain, by any means, some paintings now at the Louvre. I never suspected Mr. Somais myself, but I have suspected others —small-time operators who would seize this opportunity to get hold of the *Mona Lisa*. I've merely been waiting to see which one would rush at the bait first. Poor Poklé tried to make his own version of the *Mona Lisa* almost as valuable as the original, and he temporarily substituted it for Leonardo's painting. I foresaw that a third person would take advantage of his move. We were all afraid of one another. We all suspected one another. And we all turned out to look positively ridiculous—we journalists, these gentlemen here from the insurance company, and Mr. Somais who hates my guts!"

"You look funnier than any of us," Worson said, bursting into uproarious laughter. "Look at you in my clothes!"

"That's true. These boys even tied me up," said Cléver, taking the fake beard out of his pocket, along with the dark glasses and the little yellow cap. "My friend Alles allowed me to assume his role today. I pretended to have left Paris yesterday, and today, disguised as Worson, I intended to stay close to the unfolding events. You can see for yourselves what a fine peck of trouble I got myself into. If it hadn't been for Poklé, who released me. . . . Say, where is he?"

Suddenly everyone in the room became aware of a wisp of beard peeking through the door—the beard of a painter by the name of Poklé. Then the whole face appeared, yellow and scarred with scratches.

"Ah ha!" grunted the shipowner when he saw the painter at the door. "Thief! Traitor! You wanted to get me involved! But I didn't want the original *Mona Lisa!* I wanted the one you slapped together!"

It took a great deal of effort to pacify the agitated host, who had again experienced a terrible pain in his leg. Worson tried to explain that no one had yet been cheated in this whole affair. Moreover, added Worson, the police were very much on the alert with respect to the filming in the Louvre. Indeed, he had learned only a short while ago that, before all this trouble occurred, they had exchanged the original for a photocopy on canvas which no one could distinguish from the original or from Poklé's copy, either. What else could explain the ease with which Poklé and the insurance agents were able to take the valuable painting in and out of the museum.

Meanwhile, Jean and Michel explained to their fathers, Charles and Frédéric, that they had decided to take some revenge because for the third year in a row their fathers had reneged on their promises. At the same time the reporter took his daughter aside, and pulling out of his pocket the latest copy of *Le Clairon du Soir*, he asked her in a voice none of the others could hear, "Marie, would you know by any chance who might have sent in, under my name, an article called: 'Where's the Original *Mona Lisa?*' "

"Forgive me, Papa," said the little spy, looking as contrite as possible. "I only wanted to show you. Sometimes you think I'm a baby, that you can't take me anywhere. Yes, Father, I wrote that article, you know I did."

In the meantime, Zlatko and Koko were comforting the poor painter and giving him words of encouragement. There was no doubt that he had made a name for himself and that as soon as the shipowner had calmed down, he would buy Poklé's *Mona Lisa* for a handsome sum. The painter reached for his beard, missed it again, and cried: "Oh, my God, I almost forgot! The fake cripple! The former fake cripple! He's downstairs, at the door. Oh, by the heavenly sun up there! Of course, he's no cripple. He removed the leg and the patch from the eye. He's a great friend of all of us, and he would especially love to talk to you, Koko. He's waiting for you downstairs.

Koko looked around cautiously, scratching himself behind his ear. He didn't want to admit that he was afraid to leave the room. Zlatko gave him a fierce look, and he quickly opened the door and found himself on a poorly lit stairway.

He hadn't realized how long a flight of stairs it was. Now, although he had gone a long way, the door was still nowhere in sight. He looked back and saw the stairway stretching above him as far as he could see. He looked down and saw an infinite stairway below him. He began to run. He felt as if he had been running for hours and hours. A drop of sweat formed on the tip of his nose. Then a kind voice said from the dark, "That's the end, Koko. Wake up."

The empty corridor echoed: "Wake up!"

You have no idea what my dream is all about

29 "I knew you were crazy," Zlatko said for the
tenth time, pacing back and forth in Koko's room
and occasionally grabbing a leaf off a branch of the
locust tree that reached in through the open window.
"But I didn't know you were that crazy, I really
didn't."

Koko lay in bed, smiling, scratching behind his ear
now and then.

Koko still thought it strange that he was able to recall every minute detail of his dream. It had happened
four days earlier, on the eve of their trip to Paris. Koko's
sister had run to the kitchen to tell her mother that
Koko was still sleeping and that she couldn't wake him
up. Indeed, Koko stayed in bed that day, sweating heav-
ily and talking nonsense, saying things no one could
make head or tail of. He mentioned parrots, helicopters,
museums, and cripples, and from time to time he even
spoke in a foreign language that sounded very much

like a list of French irregular verbs. His parents called the doctor. Koko was sick for two days. The trip to Paris was postponed. And on the third day Koko told Zlatko of his exciting dream about the theft of the *Mona Lisa*. Zlatko knew that Koko could never have made up a story like that. Koko had dreamed it. And it was such an interesting dream that Zlatko kept asking his young friend to describe certain episodes over and over again. And whenever Koko repeated a portion of his story, Zlatko would pace back and forth, shake his head, and say, "I knew you were crazy, but I didn't know you were that crazy."

"But, Zlatko"—Koko would defend himself from his bed—"it was a special kind of dream. The doctor says it happens sometimes, for example, from excitement. You get so excited before taking a trip that you get sick—you grow feverish and you have all kinds of visions."

"But you should have known right away that it was a dream. I would have," Zlatko said in his cold, analytical way.

"How can you know in your dream that you are dreaming? That's why it's called a dream, for example, because you don't know it's a dream—unlike when it's not a dream and you know it isn't . . ."

"Nonsense, Koko! Listen, how come you didn't realize that you knew all those people in your dream?"

"What do you mean?" Koko asked, stunned.

"These people, they're your friends from school,

from the neighborhood, from your old home, Green Hill. For example, take that Michel Croitier. Dark hair, narrow eyes, and the way he talks. Who else is he but your next-door neighbor, Mickey Horvatich. The name's similar too—right? And the son of the fake barber Frédéric, the one with the Citroën, who smokes and has a moustache? Isn't that Ivo Branjc from Green Hill? In your dream his name is Jean Brange, but that comes to the same thing, doesn't it?"

Pale as a ghost, Koko straightened himself up in bed. He was as excited now as in the most tense moments in his dream.

"All your enemies, like Ivo and Mickey, are still your enemies in your dream. Not even their fathers were different. Ivo's father is, in fact, a barber. And your friends are even more easily recognizable. Little Marie is Marianna from your class. The same brown hair and gray eyes, and she collects photographs of actors and plays spies."

"But who's Katsarida, for example? The Greek I mean?" asked Koko softly, scratching behind his ear, his hand trembling.

"For heaven's sake, Koko, didn't you ever have a friend with green eyes who loves bicycles, who fell off his bike and broke a leg, who always reads magazines and loves photography, and whose father paints and was wounded in the leg during the war?"

"Roach!" Koko exclaimed and jumped out of bed.

"Who'd ever think that Katsarida, with such a strange name . . . ?"

"Who would indeed?" Zlatko replied. "Didn't you hear yourself saying that Katsarida was only a nickname and that it means 'insect' in Greek? Didn't you? I'll bet you *katsarida* means something like 'roach' in Greek!"

"But how can I know Greek in my dream if I don't know it when I'm awake?"

"Oh, Koko, stop that!" said Zlatko, holding his head in his hands. "That's why it's a dream. In your dream you don't know you're dreaming. That's why it's a dream because you don't know you're dreaming, unlike when you're awake and you know it."

Koko was sure that he himself had said something along those lines a while ago, but he didn't dare mention this. He got back into bed again and covered himself up to his chin. Then he remembered one more thing, and said, "You're right, Zlatko. Now I understand who the reporter is—I mean Marcel Cléver. You remember that poet Mario in Green Hill? We suspected him of being a thief. He had a cat with orange eyes. He talked to it as if it were a human being. And Maurice the butler, the gray-haired old man with a long beard, that was our friend Isaac, the old woodcutter."

"Bravo, Koko! You finally got it! Now you'll be able to figure out the rest."

"I don't know, Zlatko," Koko said carefully. "I don't

know a single painter, for example."

"You don't know a single painter! Listen, Koko, are you kidding me or are you still a little dizzy? A couple of weeks ago I loaned you a book called *You're Lying, Melita,* by Ivan Kušan. You borrowed Poklé from that book. And he paints only blue suns. And so you got the writer, whom you don't know, into your dream, and because you don't know him, you put a patch over his eye and gave him a wooden leg. Listen, Koko, you didn't even make up the parrot's name! His name was Caesar, and your dog is called Tsar . . ."

"And the actor-director?" Koko whispered. "The famous actor-director with a thick black beard?"

"Oh," Zlatko said, laughing. "That's simple enough. You changed Orson Welles into Alles Worson, just as you changed Monica Vitti to Veronica Mitty, and Peter O'Toole to Tom O'Pool. That's because you don't know anything about film actors. Ask Marianna. She'll explain everything."

Koko crawled deeper into the soft, comfortable bed. He recalled thinking in his dream how familiar Michel and Jean and Charles the barber and little Marie Cléver looked, and the rest of them as well. Yet he had thought he must be wrong because, after all, he'd never been to Paris and so he couldn't have known them. And now he felt a little sorry that his dream had been filled with so many ordinary people from his neighborhood.

"If I'd been in your place, I would have waked up a hundred times," Zlatko said. "I would have known right away I was dreaming. Listen, how could you have talked to those Parisians in French? Would you know how to say, *J'ai faim?*"

"Pardon? What did you say?" Koko asked, and suddenly feeling very timid and stupid, pulled his covers up to his eyes.

"See? You wouldn't even have known how to say 'I'm hungry.' If I hadn't known a single word of French I would have been instantly suspicious, and I'm sure I would have woken up. To say nothing of the business about *Cleopatra*."

"*Cleopatra!*" Koko cried from deep under the covers.

"If you had any brains in your head, old man, you would have remembered that the Italian painter Raphael never painted a *Cleopatra*."

The boy under the covers didn't dare admit that he had never before heard of Leonardo's *Mona Lisa* either. Meanwhile, Zlatko continued to pace back and forth, holding his head, sighing, and giving a hundred reasons why he would have woken up and thus ended this bad dream.

Koko was growing uncomfortably warm under the covers. A drop of perspiration rolled down his pointed nose, and he suddenly said boldly, "It's all your fault, Zlatko!"

"What did you say?" Zlatko was astonished and stopped in the middle of the room.

"Well, for example," Koko said, peeking out from under the covers, "you told me so many stories about

Paris, about how they fire at planes at the airport, throw you to the sharks—oh, yes, and about hunchbacked monsters that grab you. That's why I got sick!" said Koko, now with determination. "That's why I became feverish! I don't even have to go there any more. Even if I had the courage. I feel like I've been there a hundred times and like . . ."

"You have no idea what Paris is all about!" Zlatko roared, and his jaws tightened. "Once you see Paris, you won't talk such nonsense. You have no idea what Paris is all about!"

"You have no idea what my dream is all about!" Koko said sharply, wiping the sweat off his nose. "One dream like this is worth thirteen of your Parises. I don't have to travel any more. I just get into bed, pull the covers over my head, and I can go anywhere I like. To New York, to Tokyo, anyplace. And you can't! You need a train, a plane, an uncle, for example. One of my dreams is worth thirteen of your Parises."

"I knew you were crazy," said Zlatko sardonically, "but I didn't know you were that crazy."

And, slamming the door behind him, Zlatko left Koko, wondering if he might not be better off with a more intelligent travelling companion when the next opportunity arose.

And Koko pulled the covers back over his head, thinking that it might not be a bad idea to take a trip to the other end of the world that very evening.